Although generously referred to as a book by people like fairy dust, it is more of a pamphlet. I'm not enterin please don't expect literary genius.
It's nothing more than silly conversations between val gang based on their individual characters. None of the photographs were staged, they're simply snap shots of what was happening at the time. Odd moments present themselves with a regularity you could set your watch by, normally when I haven't a camera to hand.

No owls were left unsupervised with cats, I try to avoid giving them the opportunity to start a new world order involving cardboard boxes.

Who's who.

A very brief description of each member of the family and their status. Their individual characters will become apparent, many are rescues, some have been or are for release and all without exception are part of the family.

Matty.
European Eagle owl - resident.
Loves: Sitting on her chair in the corral garden, sitting like a chicken on her tree stump, sitting with her best mate Noné the cat or simply sitting.
Loathes: Hat's, sunglasses, walking sticks, fly curtains, sweet wrappers, cushions, towels, mobile phones, small children, large children, loud children, children in general and her feet being touched.

Sesi.
Alaskan Snowy owl - resident
Loves: Food, chuckling and his feet being tickled.
Loathes: Cats, bathing and he's not keen on Bob the dog.

Ella.
Tawny owl - resident.
Loves: Sleeping, stomping her feet in her owl box, bathing and having her food prepared in many and various ways depending on her whim on that particular day.
Loathes: Being woken up and flying.

Molly.
Barn owl - resident.
Loves: Bathing, swearing, doing as she wants, showing off, anything sparkly and looking in the mirror.
Loathes: Darcy and Silas the male Barn owls.

Darcy.

Black Barn owl - resident.
Loves: Food, wiggling, people from a distance and his cubby hole in the mews.
Loathes: Bathing unless his bath is in the perfect position which changes seasonally.
Silas.
Brown Breasted Barn owl - resident.
Loves: Everything and everyone particularly Molly.
Loathes: Nothing so far.
Mystic.
Northern White Faced owl - resident.
Loves: Sitting around watching life go by, food, dust bathing at 7am each morning and chick wings for breakfast.
Loathes: White dogs and orange cats.
Fuji.
Little owl - foster.
Loves: Food in vast quantities, mimicking anything, watching the CCTV monitor and beating up Houdini if he doesn't kowtow to her every whim.
Loathes: Dotty the cat and a late serving of breakfast.

Houdini.
Little owl - resident.
Loves: Hiding, sunbathing and Fuji.
Loathes: Being caught sunbathing.
Lucy.
Little owl - resident (blind).
Loves: Food, being stroked, sleeping in front of the fire, sleeping in the aviary, flying around the house from 9pm each evening, chasing cats, snuggling with cats and she adores Pixie the Maine Coon and Noné.
Loathes: Going to bed, bathing and not being allowed to get in the wood pile by the woodburner.
Schylar.
Eurasian Scops - foster.
Loves: Bathing, swinging on her swing, food and watching life go by.
Loathes: Silas the Barn owl and a late lunch.
Sasa.
Harris hawk - resident.

Loves: Food, sunbathing and squawking at people, dogs, cats and Dave the turkey.
Loathes: Having her beak and talons trimmed and she's not keen on men.
Sid & Babs.
Kookaburras - residents.
Love: Bathing, the misfortune of others, traffic, watching vapour trails from aeroplanes and foreign voices on mobile phone calls.
Loathe: Fish for lunch.

Dave.
Turkey - resident.
Loves: His own reflection, running and talking.
Loathes: Not much, he's very chilled.
Florian & Peachey.
Meerkats - residents.
Love: Eating anything out of season when it costs a fortune, people, digging, play fighting, bugs, toys, sunbathing and sleeping in their T-towel hammock on a Summer afternoon.
Loathe: Cold, rain and not quite ripe avocado pear.

Cats.

Millie: Thinks she's the boss, very demanding and unbelievably smart. Found at four weeks old by a municipal bin.
Noné: The real boss, ancient and chief cleaner of Pixie. Born here.
Pixie: The Main Coone, talks constantly, not keen on strangers or being touched and she adores Noné and GaGa. Appeared in a local advert.
GaGa: An outdoors girl, nips in and eats and then she's off again until nighttime. Washed off a roof during a storm, only days old so hand reared.
Dora: White with eyes like a sheep, disliked by all the other cats and she couldn't care less. Likes to sleep on anything white so she's often difficult to spot. Owners dumped her so she was rescued by lovely neighbours.
Pugsy: As crazy as she is fluffy, jumps over invisible lines. I witnessed her being thrown over a high wall at a petrol station by a complete moron, so I took her home.
Schminky: Part Siamese part princess. Found in a municipal bin.
Sphinx: The orange cat. Appeared and stayed.
Dotty: The baby of the family and frequently gets into trouble. Found at weeks old with dreadful cat flu which has left her with impaired vision.

Dogs.

Paddy: Laid back as long as there's a constant supply of snacks. Crawled into the car engine as a tiny puppy and fell out when I reached home, 3km away!
Nica: Deaf, half blind, touch of dementia but she can track down a piece of bread like a pro'. She came from the local dog rescue charity.
Bob: Lives to run for miles, best mate is Bestia. Another charity case.
Bestia: Multi lingual dog (Hungarian, Spanish & English). Adopted by José when just weeks old.

Released.
Pippin, Noah, Simon & Oli - Little owls.
Nettie - Nightjar.
Eddie - Eagle owl.
Katy, Kyle, Boris, Benny, Caleb, Trevor, Kevin, Gary, Jamie & Karen - Kestrels.
Luka - Lesser Kestrel.
Mungo & Midge - Field mice.
Stinky - Fox.

And a host of hedgerow birds that just needed a little help along the way.

In the Spring it's common to see hedgerow chicks in places that they shouldn't be, if they're in danger (traffic, cats, heat etc) carefully pick them up and put them somewhere that's very close by and safe, preferably high up. The parents will be within earshot and will continue to feed them.

If you have to rescue a hedgerow chick it will need warmth if it's not feathered, a hot water bottle well wrapped in towels so that the chick gets gentle heat is essential. I've always found that an old sock makes a great nest for little chicks.

Don't give it bread, you can buy great mixtures of wild bird food for fledglings in most pet shops and if the chick is very young (no feathers) just crush the mixture up and add a touch of tepid water. In an emergency get the fly swat out and go hunting.

If you can get close to a wild adult bird no matter the species there's obviously something wrong so gently catch it, put it in a box or carrier with plenty of ventilation and transport it to a vet or a rescue centre.

If it's a large bird of prey, pop a towel (or something similar) over the bird's head and body, carefully gather it up making sure its wings are tucked up against its body and watch out for the talons! Again, take it to a specialist. If for any reason you have to keep a bird of prey overnight the only safe food to offer it is raw beef, supermarket chicken has salt and chemicals which isn't ideal. Keep them cool but not cold, somewhere quiet and dark until you can get them professional help.

The art of falconry is first thought to have originated in the far east, with the first recording being as far **back as 1700 BC** . It's believed to have reached the British Isles in AD 860. While the sport was reportedly restricted to the upper classes, their lives were recorded more than the lower classes so an accurate impression is difficult to form.

In mediaeval times the bird of prey you kept indicated your status in society. The main varieties used before 1307 were the gyrfalcon, peregrine, lanner, goshawk, and sparrow-hawk; the saker, hobby, and merlin were used far less frequently for sport.

Falconry wasn't simply a sport for men, the first recorded female falconer was called Kochicu (358AD) and due to her success, falconry in Japan became widespread. Queens throughout the ages enjoyed falconry, Mary Queen of Scots had a Merlin, Queen Elizabeth I a Peregrine falcon and both were highly skilled at

hunting.

"Pixie!"
"Mmmm."
"Pix' are you awake?"
"I wasn't."
"I've got a plan."
"That's nice for you."
"No, wake up and listen, it's brilliant even if I do say it myself." Lucy's blindness never stops her scheming, or locating those that she could enlist to do the dirty work.

She sat partially on Pixie's back, fiddling her beak gently through the long silky hair which constantly needs cleaning even in mid run, mainly due to odd spots of owl spit here and there.

Pixie started to drift off to sleep again, soothed by whatever was going on behind her. After what seemed like a split second she was suddenly aware of her ear being 'groomed' with fervour, particularly the tufty bit on the tip.

"What do you want?!" It was hopeless to think that Lucy on a mission could be ignored.

"Your claws," Lucy replied, quickly.

"You've got claws of your own, why do you need mine?" Pixie knew only too well that it was almost pointless asking Lucy anything but it delayed her having to immediately get up and spring into action.

"No, you have claws and I have talons, they're completely different. Yours are retractable and mine are ready for action at all times, I can be called upon instantly to attack, catch something or even pick locks."

"Pick locks? What locks?"

"Padlocks mainly, smallish ones."

"Like the one on a shed door?" Pixie was intrigued now.

"No, a little smaller than that."

"So like a locker padlock?"

"Not quite, remember I've got to be able to get my talons right into the lock to do it." Lucy was beginning to think that she wished she'd never said anything about her skills.

"A cash box?"

"Possibly."

"A doll's house?"

"Why would anyone put a padlock on a doll's house?" asked Lucy.

"To keep them in, horrible little things with their soulless eyes and poor choice of attire. I'd lock them all in their house and then lock them in a cupboard just to make sure they couldn't escape and then throw away the key and ban you from picking the locks." Pixie scowled at the thought of zombie doll's wandering around.

"Boy, we've touched a nerve there haven't we? I never knew you didn't like doll's, they're not real you know."

"Of course they're real, I haven't just conjured up an image of a plastic, mini, replica person in my mind and called it 'a doll' they exist!" said Pixie defiantly.

"Anyway, moving on." Lucy stepped back half a step just in case Pixie decided to storm off into the kitchen as she quite often did. "Back to the plan".

"Oh yes, THE PLAN! I'd forgotten all about that," Pixie sat upright looking down at Lucy while the Little owl continued to look in the direction of where Pixie had been laying. "I'm over here Lucy."

"So you are," she said as she made a slight adjustment to 'look' at Pixie. "As you know I do like to have an adventure, nothing major we're not talking Indiana Jones or even Bear Grylls."

"More Ben Fogle then?" Pixie enquired.

"Oh definitely a Fogle type of adventure."

Little owls are very voice orientated and love a well spoken gentleman, Stephen Fry, the late great Alan Rickman, a smooth well polished tone is right up their street.

"You know the small sofa by the wood burner? Well I want to see what's underneath it but I can't get past it's sort of skirt thing that hangs down. I've tried several times, I've shuffled towards it on my knees……."

"Have you got knees?" Pixie interrupted.

"Of course I've got knees! How do you think I can sit down without having a set of knees?"

"I thought you just flopped forwards or backwards then when you wanted to get up you flapped your wings."

"Obviously you were in the top of the biology class! All birds have knees and before you say it, even penguins have them as well."

"Oh OK, I stand corrected." replied Pixie.

"So back to the sofa, I need you to lift its skirt up so I can get underneath. I've seen you lie on your back doing it before so if you can repeat that performance, we can get started". Lucy jumped down onto the floor with a vague flap of her wings.

"If you say so. You know this won't go down well if we get caught," Pixie cautioned.

"Don't be such a scaredy Coone!" Replied Lucy with a snigger as she prepared to go into the unknown, under the sofa.

The plan worked like a dream, Pixie expertly lifted the draping front skirt panel of the settee and Lucy scrambled into the gloom.

"What can you see?"

"Oh that's funny!"

"You know what I mean, what can you sense then?" Pixie corrected her faux pas quickly.

"I think there's one of your toy mice here, I'll drag it out for you." After a little huffing and puffing a bright pink toy mouse appeared looking somewhat worse for wear. Beneath every sofa is where dust and cat hair go to live when they grow up and leave home and the mouse had welcomed the elements into its string whiskers.

"Ewwww!" Pixie recoiled from the toy immediately and let go of the material she'd been employed to hold aloft."Is there anything else?"

"No, not much. Hang on a minute, I think this is a pen," replied Lucy shuffling around under the back of the sofa.

"As neither of us can write I'd leave that there," said Pixie, she was starting to get a little bored with this so-called adventure.

"Mystic can write" Lucy piped up excitedly "we can give it to her." Out came the pen in due course.

"Where's Lucy, Pix'?"

"Lucy! We've been caught."

"I know, I heard her. I'm not sure which way is out".The Little owl began scrambling this way and that under the sofa but making no headway at all.

"Quick!"

"Pixie! Where's Lucy? Oh no she's not under the sofa!!!" This was just the sort of thing one doesn't need thrown into the mix of a busy day.

"Yeah, she sort of is a bit," Pixie replied sheepishly.

"Oh for goodness sake, how can you two get into so much mischief in such a short time? I was only answering an email". I walked across the room at which point Pixie disappeared into the kitchen.

With that the sectional sofa had to be gingerly taken apart after crawling around on my hands and knees to see exactly where Lucy had positioned herself. Bit by bit she was uncovered in all her dusty glory. Cleaned off, told off and returned to her basket in front of the fire.

"We got away with that one nicely Pix', a quick dust down and blah, blah, blah. Could have been worse," Lucy was looking rather smug as she ruffled her feathers into place and settled down for a snooze.

"What I don't get is why you wanted to go under there in the first place," replied Pixie.

"Pugsy said that there was a treasure trove of mealworms kept under the sofa for emergencies."

"And you listened to Pugsy? This is the cat that jumps over invisible lines and gets her head stuck in jugs! She's hardly reliable on any level," Pixie couldn't believe her ears and Pugsy is shall we say a little special.

"Aaaah there's no harm done, in fact we did her a good turn pointing out all that debris under the sofa. She had the hoover out and everything, nice and clean now."

Lots of falconry terms are still used in everyday

English:

Under the thumb - To hold the jesses under your thumb in order to control the bird of prey.

At the end of your tether - A tether is what's used to secure a bird of prey to its outdoor perch.

Fed up - When a bird of prey has eaten it's fill and goes to sleep.

Hoodwinked - To hood a bird for hunting purposes.

Bated breath - When a bird of prey 'bates' from its perch it waits for the falconer to put it on the perch again and can often be breathing heavily from the exertion.

Haggard - A bird of prey caught from the wild during migration (thankfully now illegal to do).

Cadge - A portable perch which falconers would use to transport the bird of prey hence 'to cadge a lift'.

Boozer - When raptors drink it's called bowsing. A bird drinking a lot of water is called a 'boozer'.

Wrapped around your little finger - To wrap the jesses around your finger for extra security when holding a hunting bird.

Eyes like a hawk - Not only can hawks see greater distances than humans, but their visual acuity (the ability to see clearly) is eight times that of ours.

Rouse - When a bird shakes its feathers before taking off is called 'to rouse up'.

"What are you up to Mystic?" I asked, noticing her staring at the tablet on the dining table.

"I'm entering a competition. If I tell you what to write, can you type it in for me? I'm struggling to do it with my talons, they keep slipping on the screen".

"Yes, of course I can. So what have you got to do to enter?" I replied while polishing the table around her. There's always something to do and if multitasking is possible then I go for that option.

"I've got to come up with a short poem about owls, that's what caught my attention really," said Mystic, gazing out of the patio doors for inspiration.

"Oh, well that's topical isn't it, have you thought of anything?"

'There was a young owl from Southend'
'Who spoke every word that she penned'
'She chittered and chattered'

'Giggled and cackled'
'And was never short of a friend'
'She wrote all the time'
'In foul weather or fine'
'Using up pages'
'And all of her wages'
'Which amounted to only one dime'

"Very good Myst', do you want me to type that for you?"

From an owlet Mystic had always been the most creative and articulate out of all the owls, though small in stature she made up for it in determination and could often be seen gripping a pen, mind you her writing style left a lot to be desired.

"Yes please, if you don't mind." Mystic took a step back from the tablet to give me enough space.

"So if you win the competition, what's the prize?" I asked as I started to type out the poem onto the entry page.

"A hang glider," she replied casually.

"But you can fly, you don't need a hang glider. You've got wings."

"Yes I know, I'd sell it and buy a new phone and an Alexa so that I could listen to things I like rather than having to listen to the rubbish you have playing."

"I don't listen to rubbish, I'll have you know Fleetwood Mac are timeless!"

"Hopeless, more like, all that wailing it curls my feathers!"

"You've just got no taste Mystic, that's your problem."

"No, quite the opposite in fact. I do have taste and it doesn't lean towards out of date hippy singers!"

That was me put in my place, we're still waiting to hear if Mystic has won a hang glider. The closing date is 2025, another *Reader's Digest* special.

Scops Owls are easily preyed on because of their small size. For this reason, they have developed some physical and behavioural adaptations that help them blend into their environment, thus remaining unnoticed to potential predators.

Their camouflaging plumage is one aspect; in addition to which they will stretch their bodies to look leaner and sway back and forth to appear even more like a tree branch moving in a breeze.

Their calls consist of a series of whistles or high-pitched hoots, given with a frequency of 4 calls per second or less, or a single, drawn-out whistle.

The calls differ between species in type and pitch, Mystic can purr like a cat or if alarmed she coo's like a dove.

Scops owls are generally insectivorous feeding on a wide range of insects; however, depending on the species, they may take small birds, small mammals - such as bats and mice - as well as earthworms, amphibians and aquatic invertebrates.

Most hunting is done from an open perch in semi-open areas with old trees with hollows. When they spot prey, they drop down catching them either on the ground or flying insects are caught mid-air.

Their excellent sense of hearing and sight help them locate prey; and their well-developed raptorial claws and curved bills, are efficient tools for tearing their prey into pieces small enough for

them to swallow easily.

"I don't know what the world is coming to," said Tio. He'd seen 19 years come and go so had a wealth of experience to draw upon, although his parlance was distinctively alike to Eeyore from ' *Winnie The Pooh'*.
"Oh, I know what you mean, it's a disaster." Noné was no spring chicken herself at 14 years old but a completely different character. The greatest foster mum to anything she could clean. Whether they were furred or feathered she'd look after them. Many an owlet had been subjected to being cleaned with her rough tongue, after the first couple of times it became the norm' and they'd wait patiently while she gave them a firm yet very gentle wash.
"You can say that again!" replied Tio.

"You've got this bloody pandemic sweeping across the world, people dropping like flies all over the place, poor souls. Businesses closing, people being furloughed and made redundant. They're all having to wear masks you know. Whenever they go out anywhere they have to mask up. It's not right. And what are the governments doing about it? That's what I'd like to know. Making up their own rules the same as always, one rule for them and another rule for everyone else. It's bloody shameful, it really is. What about all the elderly people living alone, nobody to talk to, frightened to go out. Then there's the youngsters, they've been off school, home taught, can't have friends over, it's all a right pickle." Noné paused to take a breath and before Tio could get a word in she was off again.

"Then there's the Saharan storms we've had, bloody pink sand everywhere. You can't go out 'cos it gets in your eyes and trying to get it out of fur is as easy as juggling chainsaws! GaGa is plastered in the stuff, not that she worries about it. The weather's gone mad, no rain for months, the lake is half the size it was. I remember when we used to have snow, a week in December followed by a couple of days in January, always the same every year. There's not been a flake in this area for at least five years, they get it on the coast now. Snow on the beach!"

"Oh yeah, I forgot about all of that."

"What were you talking about then?" Facing Tio now, Noné gave him a quizzical look.

"They've changed the Felix cat food packets to light blue, it looks dreadful!"

A tiny wee boy, quite simply just fluff,
Jumped in front of the car,
Right out of the rough,
As black as night skies,
With green eyes a gander,
His teeth were on loan,
From a semi retired vampire,
They shone in the dark,
Scaring the ghosts,
Twenty years by my side,
He had something to boast.
RIP Lovely Tio.

"What the hell is that?!" For one of the largest species of owls on the planet she really was in the back of the queue when pluckiness was dished out.

"What's, what Matty?" I asked.

"Up there, that!"

"I can't see what you're looking at".

"That! That thing up there, swinging around!"

"I still can't see it," along with her standard of courage was my ever decreasing vision. I'd even employed the wrinkling nose and slightly gaping mouth which for no known reason is meant to give you 0.00006% better chance of spotting something. In reality you don't actually have to make any ridiculous faces at all, you can't see any clearer even if contorted.

"Open your bloody eyes! That black thing, spiralling towards me." Matty said, shuffling from foot to foot which she always did when nervous.

"What, that?" I pointed from a distance towards whatever it was. The object of our interest was merrily caught in a slight breeze and blowing around on what looked like the end of a silken thread. "It's probably a tiny spider."

"Yeah the 'pider', that thing. Get it away from me!"

"It won't hurt you. I bet it's more frightened of you, than you are of it."

"Wanna put money on that? It's got huge pointy teeth and they're gnashing right in my direction, those on top of it's manic grin. It's freaking me right out!"

"It hasn't got huge teeth."

"I'm telling you it's like a shark! Remember, I can see four billion times better than humans and at least a zillion times better than you peering through your glasses, which incidentally have more scratches than a flea bitten hound."

"Stop exaggerating, your eyesight is amazing but………..".

"For crying out loud, quit the wittering and do something, it's nearly on me!"

"I haven't got anything to put it in." I replied, looking around for a glass or jar.

"I don't want to keep it as a bloody pet! Get something to swipe it with."

"Like what?"

"There's a Little owl over there, hit it with that".

"I'm not going to hit it with Pippin! I'll snap a twig off one of the bushes and move it that way."

"What sort of twig?"

"Does it matter?"

"Of course it matters, I don't want leaves thrust in my face as well as the 'pider'. Get one without any leaves or flowers. Can this day get any worse?!"

"You are such a drama queen. Look, I've got a bit of rosemary to put it on."

"Oh no, not rosemary, it stinks."

"You have no sense of smell, how do you know it stinks?"

"The orange cat piddles up it, I'm not stupid".

"Oh, you could have told me before I snapped a sprig off. Thank goodness I've been using the other bush for cooking."

"I was too busy watching the thing, you can't take your eyes off 'em otherwise they disappear and not knowing where they are is even worse. Oh and by the way the orange cat visits the other rosemary bush on the bank, nothing's sacred."

"Where is it now?"

"Right here, in front of my chest. Get a move on!"

"Matty it's not a spider, it's a knot on the end of some cotton that's hanging down from the shade sail, you banana."

"A knot? But it's got teeth, I could see its teeth!"

"It's the end of the cotton, just a tiny tuft coming out of the knot. So much for your incredible eyesight hey?"

"Well you can't be too careful, it's better to err on the side of caution I always say." She ruffled her feathers to indicate that the state of alarm had now been dropped.

"I would suggest it's better to see what you're dealing with before getting your knickers in a twist to be honest."

"That's easy for you to say, it wasn't coming towards you."

"Matty, why didn't you just move out of the way? One flap and you would have been in another part of the garden."

"I didn't think of that" she replied, settling down for a well earned

snooze in the cool Spring sunshine.

European or Eurasion Eagle owls have an average life span of 20 years when living in the wild. The oldest wild specimen that was found from this species, was estimated to be almost 28 years. In contrast, they triple their life span when they are in managed captivity like zoos, with some birds surviving up to 68 years.

"What an absolutely stonking night, I'm bloody knackered!" Although of senior years now Paddy the short arsed version of a Labrador was still the ring leader when it came to mischief.

"Yeah, I could do with a kip. Those foxes know how to party don't they?" Replied Bob, the baby of the pack.

"Always a good knees up with the old 'Vulpes', they're such a bloody laugh but you've got to keep your wits about you. Big practical jokers that lot," Bestia, by far the most intelligent, also multilingual (Hungarian, Spanish & English) and had a slightly annoying habit of casually dropping in a smidge of Latin where he could.

"Did you see them stick Geoff in that barrel? Poor sod," said Paddy as he threw himself backwards into the Esparto grass.

"Which Geoff, him with the crooked tail?" Bob asked.

"No, Geoff - Geoff, him with the cleft palate. Always has to drink water from a bowl on a chair otherwise it comes out his nose. I know I shouldn't, but it makes me laugh every time he drinks from the river."

"Oh him, no I missed that 'cos Ronnie was telling us a joke."

' A man walks into a restaurant with a full-grown ostrich behind him. The waitress asks for their orders. The guy says, "A hamburger, fries, and a coke," and turns to the ostrich, "What's yours?"
"I'll have the same," says the ostrich.
A short time later the waitress returns with the order. "That will be 18.40 € please."
The man reaches into his pocket and, without looking, pulls out the exact change for payment.

The next day, the guy and the ostrich return to the same restaurant and the guy says, "A hamburger, fries, and a coke."
The ostrich says, "I'll have the same."
Again the guy reaches into his pocket and pays with exact change. This becomes routine until one night they enter the restaurant and the waitress asks, "The usual?"
"No, this is Friday night, so I will have a steak, baked potato, and salad", says the guy.
"Me too," says the ostrich.
The waitress brings the order and says, "That will be 42.62 €."
Once again the guy pulls the exact change out of his pocket and places it on the table.
The waitress can't hold back her curiosity any longer. "Excuse me, sir. How do you manage to always come up with the exact change out of your pocket every time?"
"Well," says the guy, "several years ago I was cleaning my attic and found an old lamp. When I rubbed it a genie appeared and offered me two wishes. My first wish was that if I ever had to pay for anything, I would just put my hand in my pocket and the right amount of money would always be there."
"That's brilliant!" says the waitress. "Most people would wish for a million Euro or something, but you'll always be as rich as you want for as long as you live!"
"That's right. Whether it's a packet of crisps or a Rolls Royce, the exact money is always there," says the guy.
The waitress asks, "But, sir, what's with the ostrich?"
The guy sighs and answers, "My second wish was for a tall chick with long legs who agrees with everything I say."
The dogs fall about laughing, Paddy holding his portly sides to stop them

wobbling out of control.

Esparto grass was formerly used in cordage, for producing paper paste, tissues and crafts, especially basketry. It has also been used in naval carpentry for the necessity to seal the boards of the ship hulls.

Nowadays a few people still prepare products made of esparto like shoes, baskets and of course donkeys for the artisan markets but there appears to be a revival.

Once a dying trade, the younger generations didn't want to harvest the grass any more, it's back aching work for little recompense. Some town halls occasionally would run weaving classes in the hope that the craft could be passed down the generations.

A company in Porcuna (Jaen) established in 1957 has been creating traditional items with a modern twist. Perez y Perez a family owned business not only creates fabulous esparto bulls and cacti for the home design world but also curtains, umbrellas, awnings and even room sets.

Using techniques almost unchanged from the Neolithic period, esparto baskets of over seven thousand years old have been discovered in cave houses in Granada, this sustainable grass with its vegan credentials is on the brink of global endorsement. Chemical free, hard wearing and after many years of use it can then be shredded to fertilise the land.

Esparto window blinds can now be seen all over the world in hot countries,
providing shade, noise reduction and they're also a fly repellent.

     These two are hilarious together. Noné is partially deaf through old age and Pugsy is partially daft so their exchanges are normally quite surreal in content and often confusing to the outside world.

     "What d'you reckon?" Noné said, looking out over the valley.

     "Reckon, 'bout what?" The reply from Pugsy came several seconds after the question, she was never that speedy at anything so it made sense that everyone always had to wait a little for a reaction.

     "D'you want to go for a stroll through the valley? We could go down to the big river at the bottom and see if there are any voles kicking around."

     Saliva started to gather in her mouth as Noné mused on water voles, she imagined them as if they were in a circus. 'Roll up, roll up ladies and gentlemen, boys and girls, step right up! Come and see the amazing voles, they'll thrill you with their acrobatical accomplishments as they fly through the air......................' And straight into my mouth Noné thought.

     "Yeah, could do. What about going over the stream though? I'm really not that keen on anything moving beneath me, it makes me feel a bit queasy," Pugsy looked at the irrigation channel below. This would be the first theoretical hurdle but there was a small bridge made from a scaffold plank so it wasn't as if they had to jump over.

     "Makes you feel cheesy? Is that not a good thing? Nothing wrong with a bit of cheese, not that they let us have any, keep it all to themselves they do."

"Not cheesy, queasy. I don't like the water running under the bridge, I always think I'm going to fall in," explained Pugsy with an even slower delivery than normal.

"Oh right, I see what you're saying. They'll be turning the water off this morning so we could wait until then. Would that make you happier?"

"I can't answer that in truth Noné on the grounds that I'm not in possession of a rational response". She had a point, Pugsy had run it through her limited thought capacitors and nothing had flagged up. This happened with regularity but she'd learnt to accept it and of course the invisible lines that popped up all over the place. "How do they switch the water off then?"

"It's a big tap, they turn it and no more water comes out".

"What like a bath tap?"

"Well not quite, but good enough for now." Noné had settled herself down for the long haul, carrying a little too much weight on old paws she took every opportunity to rest these days. The pine needles under the tree made for a very comfy bed in absence of a scrunched up newspaper, cardboard box or freshly ironed white blouse. Pugsy copied the idea and soon they were curled up side by side still gazing across the open countryside.

"So where's this big tap?" Pugsy could see a large shining tap in her mind's eye but couldn't quite recall if she'd seen it anywhere in real life. She often strolled through the olive groves and down to the river and thought that surely she'd have seen a huge silvery object marked with a capital C (for cold of course) somewhere along the way.

"Aah, well I'm not one hundred percent sure but there was a programme all about it with that Joanna woman, you know the one with blonde hair." As an avid TV fan Noné had gleaned much information on all manner of things over the years, not all had been understood or remembered but she did appear to others to be the fount of all knowledge.

"The one that's all posh like?"

"No not Posh Spice, she was a model and an actress centuries ago in the 80's. Anyway this lady went to the source of the irrigation in a boat with a man who spoke another language, must have been Spanish I suppose as it was around here somewhere."

"Two of them in a boat? Are they 'Borrowers'? You'd be hard pressed to fit a rubber duck on our irrigation channel let alone a boat!" Pugsy said with far more animation than was usually available to her.

"Well a canoe then, I don't know but they didn't swim there because of the crocodiles." Noné was starting to wish she'd kept her mouth shut on the subject.

"Crocodiles! We've got bloody crocodiles here, in the water?" Immediately springing to her feet Pugsy's eyes were drawn down to the water below, a soupçon of adrenaline began to wade through her veins. All the times she'd gone to sleep by the river, the sound of the water lulling her into a peaceful dream filled slumber and she could have been snapped up. Literally!

"No, they don't come this far down. They tend to stay near to the tap end as far as I know, more space there for doing whatever they do like catching antelopes and such like". Noné was beginning to flounder now, she couldn't quite remember all the details of Miss.Lumley's experience in finding the source but she had at that precise moment recalled where it had been discovered.

"Africa! That's where they turn the water off."
"Where's that then?"
"It's where the river goes over the road, just beyond the olive grove there." Pointing it out to Pugsy, Noné decided that she was rapidly becoming hungry. Without looking back she sauntered away in search of the food bowl in the kitchen leaving Pugsy to stare in the direction of Africa and the source of the Nile...........Where the big tap is.

Pugsy didn't have the best of starts in life.

Dumped at a petrol station in Almeria when she was just a few weeks old, the
petrol attendant tried to keep her safe and always made sure she was well
fed.

One day a vile man picked the sleeping kitten up from a chair and hurled her
over a nearby wall onto concrete 3m below. Having witnessed this I ran to where the kitten landed and gathered her up, dazed and bleeding. With the encouragement of the petrol attendant I took the kitten with me.

Her cuts and bruises healed quickly but it became apparent that she had a few foibles, probably from the head injury but she's happy and healthy which is all important.

This week, as I write, Pugsy has decided that her tail doesn't belong to her. She's momentarily alarmed if she catches sight of it and has decided not to clean it ever again. She's a special girl.

"I mean really, did you honestly believe those would enhance any outfit? They're offensive!"

Mystic has always loved shoes, it's the first thing she looks at when meeting somebody new and she keeps a constant check on who's wearing what everyday. It's like living with Miranda Priestly from ' *The Devil Wears Prada* ', fortunately apart from this fetish she's very non judgemental on apparel.

"So let me get this straight, you got up this morning and decided that the best things to put on your feet were great big clomping boots. Bearing in mind the rest of your ensemble, cut off jeans and a T-shirt with a 3D upside down fruit bat on it."

"In my defence Mystic, not that it's any of your business they're walking boots because I'm taking you lot for a walk this morning." I replied, trying not to get embroiled in yet another shoe based discussion.

"So you're unable to walk in those nice red baseball boots which quite frankly would coordinate with the red writing on your T shirt, bring the whole lot together?" Mystic was still staring at my boots as though revolted yet mesmerised at the same time. "Or the grey pumps with poppies on them, they'd do at a push."

"I'm not mincing down a catwalk Myst', I'm going to be walking out in the countryside over pebbles, in mud and probably jumping across irrigation channels with an owl on my glove. I don't think a pair of pumps will cut it to be honest with you." For me the debate was near a close but from her continued scrutiny she was nowhere near finished.

"Well if you must wear those things, get rid of the shorts," she replied.

"So I should just walk along the road and through the valley in my knickers? I don't really think that's the best idea, do you?" I could hear the annoyance creeping into my voice but at a glacial pace, this was one of a thousand conversations that had been centred on my choice of attire on any given morning. I was experienced in this field, I could hold my own.

"Don't be ridiculous, I meant change into some jeans. That way the boots won't look so huge attached to your skinny legs, you look like something a child would draw." A smirk reached her beak as she realised what she'd said, I could see her creating the image in her mind of me as a caricature with legs of string and gigantic black blobs at the end of each.

"It's far too warm for jeans and I can't stand here all day discussing foot wear, I've got to get Matty out for a walk before it's too hot." I went into the mews to get the big girl out, she was ready and waiting for her ramble through the pine forest. "At least you don't mind what I'm wearing do you?"

"Nah". Matty's conversational grasp at 7am was always littered with one syllable words, her vocabulary didn't normally drag itself out of bed until lunchtime which made for very relaxed exchanges as long as the questions could be answered by 'nah'.

As we passed Mystic's basket in the corral garden, she had the look of a mother who had, had the last word. If it were at all possible her beak would have been pursed. Matty gave her a 'nah' as I opened the corral door and Mystic reacted as usual by turning into a grey stick like creature with slitty eyes - They're not called transformer owls for nothing.

Negotiating myself, Matty and my gargantuan boots out of the doorway I closed the door to Matty passing comment to Mystic.

"I would have thought she'd have worn the green hiking boots, they slim her feet down a treat." Everyone's a critic!

In this household there's no clear line between religion and curtain length.

Lucy the 'visually challenged' owl and Pixie the smallest Maine Coon in the world spend much of their time together in the evenings, discussing all manner of topics.

"Do you know you're behind the curtain." Pixie felt the need to point it out just in case Lucy hadn't been aware, she presumed that Lucy's overall experience with soft furnishings may have been quite limited.

"Yes, of course I know I'm behind a curtain." The reply was a little terse, Pixie thought, but she was used to Lucy's occasional snappy demeanour.

"What are you doing behind the curtain?"

"I'm just penning a quick sonnet! What do you think I'm doing here?"

"Alright huffy pants, you can drop the attitude I was only asking as you have a lighter at your feet so I was a bit concerned about your motives. We've had one fire here and that was enough to last several lifetimes."

"If you must know I'm getting undressed so some privacy wouldn't go amiss, if you don't mind." Lucy turned her back towards Pixie as if to hammer home her requirements.

"How can you get undressed? You don't wear any clothes. Have you been dressing up in cobwebs again?"

"There comes a time each year when all birds have to get undressed and then some more feathers appear, it's all very simple so even you should be able to follow that." As haughty as you like Lucy continued with what she was doing.

Appearing from behind the curtain with a flourish Lucy held a wing feather in her beak like a trophy.

"What are you going to do with that now?" Pixie asked, hoping that it would be a two minute focus on playtime. She loved feathers.

"Oh it's going on Ebay for the weird and wonderful crowd, they love owl feathers you know. Spells and potions, wafting and weaving. There's a whole host of 'em out there that will snap this up at a reasonable price."

"That's fantastic! I never knew you sold them, is that how you managed to get the lighter?" Pixie was genuinely impressed by the Little owls business acumen, she had no idea that Lucy even had an Ebay account or what Ebay was.

"Oh that, no I'm building a gas barbecue. I quite fancy some jerk chicken at the weekend."

Sometimes Lucy lost Pixie with some of her advanced ways and ideas, she was such a city slicker having come all the way from Huercal Overa and it's bright lights and gold paved streets.

Little owls in particular, have an odd way of moulting their feathers.

If you've ever watched *Harry Potter and the Chamber of Secrets* you will have seen The Whomping Willow shed all of its leaves at once in the Autumn, that gives you a clue as to how Little owls do it.

One day they've got a tail, the next day it's fallen out. The only real clue to their intention to change their feathers is their insatiable appetite for the week leading up to it. Obviously they can't fly with only 50% feather coverage, so they eat everything in sight and then sit around for a couple of days waiting for their new wardrobe to arrive.

They also get a bit moody as well, so best to steer clear of a moulting Little owl if you don't want to have abuse hurled at you.

    When I was a young whippersnapper of a kit life seemed simpler, ideals were firm and things to live up to. Schooling provided not only education but social interaction and furnished us with the tools one would require in later years.

    Mind you from an early age I did consider myself a bit of a trailblazer and had my heart set on becoming an intergalactic unicorn, my parents never really encouraged that, of course these days that lack of parental support would be seen as neglect.

    It seems in this day and age kits can do just as they please, have what they want and still demand more.

    I remember when I had to get up at the crack of dawn, the dim light of sunrise barely visible. Breakfast would be a beetle if I was lucky, a woodlouse if not quite so fortunate and I'd polish either off in a second. As soon as breakfast was over I'd be told to start the guard shift so that the rest of the family could eat, we meerkats really have to keep a close eye out for airborne attacks.

Once I spotted a hang glider, even from the ground I could see the glint in his eyes and the way he was coming around to enter into a dive. No doubt he was after our food, they can be a funny crowd these extreme sportsmen and women. It's all about high protein intake and he obviously was weighing up whether he could rob our meal worm stash.

I let out a warning bark to alert the rest of the family, within a split second they were by my side and we were united against the floating foe. We barked in unison until we could bark no more (for about a minute in truth as we do get sidetracked or bored quite quickly). With a swish barely audible to humans but like the sound of a rocket to us the glider changed his route, obviously frightened by the powerful image we portrayed. Not many would take on a mob of 6 meerkats if they were wise!

Anyway I've digressed from how hard done by we were as children.

After the guard duty and everyone had eaten we were then put to work, various chores had to be done daily from housework to tunnel excavation. You human people don't realise how busy we are! Each day we have to clean out the bunker, specially the nursery wing as that can get notably whiffy as you can imagine, never my favourite task working in there.

I much preferred digging tunnels, we dug new ones each day or improved on those that had become a little shabby. You could really get your paws into to it unless it had been raining, then the mud would just form huge clods making it impossible to walk without everyone wetting themselves with laughter.

The day also held such delights as scavenging for bugs, grooming each other, fighting, playing and continual guard duty. Once night fell we'd all stumble into the bunker exhausted and the moment our heads hit the hay we'd be fast asleep.

They were hard days, but happy ones. There was none of this namby, bloody pamby nonsense, getting up at midday because of spending the night playing computer games. Obviously we have ethernet in the bunker now, one has to keep up to date with modern technology and we do enjoy a bit of 'Facetime' with relatives of course but lights out means just that!

I've heard that kits today just sit around on their mobiles Tik Toking, Instagraming, Twittering and using the rest of social media platforms that in my personal opinion are creating absolute zombies, so much so they design zombie games to appease the masses. It's a never ending vicious circle.

Bring back child labour! Get the little tikes washing the dishes, sweeping the floor, doing the laundry or preparing food, guide them to adulthood with all the aptitude they'll require to survive and bring their own family up.

Ooh National Service, that would sort the bugga's out!

Darcy - Cortijo Búho

Darcy is special, not just because he's a Black Barn Owl but he's not the brightest light in the harbour, a twist short of a slinky, basically he has an intellect only rivalled by kitchen utensils but he is adorable in every way.

"Come on Darcy, let's go for a walk". He looked at me from his perch in the mews without any expression at all, which of course was completely normal.

"I've only got little legs" he'd made a good point.

"No little mate, you're not walking I'll do the walking" I replied.

"Ok. See you later." With that Darcy closed his eyes again to return to the land of nod. Barn Owls, like cats do spend 99% of their time asleep or staring into the middle distance is another favourite pastime.

I went into the enclosure to put on his 'furniture' which is what the soft leather anklets and jesses are called.

"Are we going out somewhere?" Darcy asked as he jumped onto the glove.

"No Darcy, I thought we'd sit and discuss the basic concept of nuclear fusion. However if you'd prefer to go for a walk then we could do that instead". I was feeling pretty confident that he'd not opt for the talk.

"I like the walk thing more than the 'knickerly fashion', I don't know what that is but it doesn't sound very interesting". Darcy moved to his prefered standing position on the glove which of course is backwards and we set off.

"Who are they?" He asked as we walked out of the gate.

"The dogs, Paddy the short, fat Labrador, Sneaky Nica, Bob & Bestia, the same dogs as yesterday and the day before that" I replied.

"So they're always here?"

"Well Paddy and Nica arrived about ten years ago and they don't show any signs of moving out, Bob was a poor abandoned puppy so he joined us last year and Bestia is José's dog." This was a daily conversation but Darcy then went off on a tangent.

"Why do they have four legs? I only have two, you have two, the ducks and chickens have two.........." Luckily Darcy ran out of comparisons at that point otherwise he would have named every creature on earth with two legs. One thing about this little owl was his ability to format questions, one of his best being if 'someone owns a piece of land, do they own it all the way to the centre of the earth?'

"They need four legs for proper weight distribution, can you imagine Fat Paddy standing on his hind legs? He'd sink into the ground with all of those kilos weighing down on his little paws." I'd hoped that would be the end of it as I really didn't have any other answers.

"Mystic has huge feet and she doesn't weigh very much," Darcy replied accurately.

"Mmm, well we don't normally point out her huge feet or her moustache for that matter. We're all different Darcy, look at you for example you're a Barn owl but you're black when you should be white."

"I'm black?! When did that happen?" The little fella had made a joke.

We walked on in relative silence, Darcy still backwards on the glove looking at what we'd passed with very few comments apart from a low growl at two Choughs sat on an old tree stump, they are a gobby pair though with their jibes and quite shocking language sometimes.

Having reached our 3km point we started to head for home. Darcy piped up with a topic he'd obviously been pondering on.

"Why doesn't Paddy have hooves?" I could see where he was coming from immediately, Paddy did have the girth of a pig. Perhaps little Darcy isn't as daft as we thought.

Although the overuse of exclamation marks is often the sign of an unsound mind that certainly doesn't apply to Lucy the Little Owl.

She has for some unknown reason taken a dislike to the popular TV presenter Sandi Toksvig who is indeed vertically challenged as she freely remarks on herself. So one would think Lucy would hold her in much higher esteem being on the short side herself.

As a fanatical fan of Stephen Fry who presented QI before Sandi took over. She would sit still through the whole programme (which is quite long in a Little owls timescale), not a 'bee-bop' would be heard from her until the titles rolled at the end of the show.

So it was that one evening we settled down for a bit of light hearted banter and interesting facts that immediately vacate one's mind the moment they're aired. Lucy was in position in front of the screen, after all her eyesight is impaired and she's the size of a Granny Smith apple so it would be inexcusable to expect her to sit behind me.

The opening sequence with its well known musical accompaniment started, Lucy fluffed her feathers in readiness to settle down and watch Mr. Fry host the show in his convivial style but to her horror he wasn't there!!!!!

Instead a small blonde apparition sat in the big chair barely able to see over the desk. Worst was yet to come, Sandi spoke!!! Lucy spun around to look at me.

"WHO IS THAT?!"

As a long standing fan of Sandi I did try to explain what a talented (albeit miniature) lady she is but it was falling on deaf, feathered ears. Lucy wasn't impressed and she'd had enough, just five minutes into the show she gently took off like a battery powered fairy (which could do with recharging) in search of Pixie.

One has to admire the steely determination of a Little Owl, we have not sat together and watched QI since that night back in November 2019 although these days she sometimes takes in an episode of 'Would I Lie To You' - It's a Sandi free show.

I don't take orders, I barely take suggestions!
You know the day is going to be a little amiss when although it's Wednesday it feels like a Sunday.

Molly the Barn Owl is a diva, she knows it and we know it. She's a spectacular flyer, precise in every landing, almost obsessive in her presentation and a handful when she's in a bad mood. You wouldn't think that owls have good or bad moods but believe me they all do and Molly can turn into a demon if everything is not to her liking.

Every morning when the mews is opened up we say good morning to each of the birds and all but Molly respond, she normally opens one eye and promptly closes it again. If you linger by her enclosure she'll drop her head down and move it from side to side as if saying no. Or if it's the day from hell she'll swear like a trouper, sounding like a raging kettle on the boil.

So it was one Wednesday morning that I opened the mews at 6am, greeted all the birds and quickly passed by Molly to avoid waking her up before 10am, that was the earliest she would respond with anything other than wrath.

A couple of hours later once the sun had come up it was time for the birds to go out into the garden where they could sit and watch the world go by, snooze and have some fresh air. Of course Molly still wasn't stirring but it was such a beautifully warm start to the day, I took my chances.

"Mol' are you getting up?"

"What would Beyoncé say," came her reply as she kept her eyes tightly shut but you knew she was rolling them behind her lids.

"I think you'd find Beyoncé giving an uplifting speech about empowering women, the importance of being independent and working hard. Does that answer your question Molly?" Her eyes snapped open with the speed of a politician's promise on election day.

"But it's Sunday and we usually get to choose what we want to do on a Sunday, that's all I meant." This was delivered with a silky, sulky note that really didn't cut any ice with me at all.

"It's not Sunday Molly, it's Wednesday and you are going to sit in the garden and enjoy it. Everyone else is out, napping in the warm breeze and it will do you good to join them."

"It can't be Wednesday, where have the rest of the days gone? If you're correct that means I've missed out on two walks, you know I like going through the pine forest and flying across the fields. That's my favourite!" Seriously stroppy now, Molly was starting to wind up in a big style.

"It's been raining Mol' and we all know you don't 'do' rain so you slept through it apart from eating, even then I don't think you were fully awake." I was trying to appeal to her better nature, she's a very savvy girl when all's said and done. It's just a case of finding that trait in her personality where you can reason with her, mind you that task in itself can be like trying to blow out a lightbulb.

"Well don't just stand there dithering, get me out!" I did as I was told and opened the door to her enclosure fully expecting her to jump on to my glove as she normally did. WRONG! She pushed past me and stormed out of the mews into the garden like a raging bull.

"What are you doing Molly?"

"Well, unlike Beyoncé I don't have two dozen personal trainers to keep me fit and if all I've been doing is sleeping and eating for days on end then I've gone too fat so I can't bloody fly. Can I? It's all your fault you should have woken me up earlier!"

Often one can't do right for doing wrong, all the time.

I had my patience tested, I'm negative!

"Raaaaahhhhh, what d'you want?!"

"Just to walk past really Sasa, I didn't expect you to kick off with such fervour to be honest." Sasa (or Sha' as she's known) was sitting on her tree stump opposite Sydney and Babs (the kookaburras) enclosure, her normal spot where she could hurl abuse at them and anyone or anything else that caught her beady eye. This time it appeared to be me.

"It wasn't meant for anyone in particular, I was just trying it out. I've felt recently that I've sounded wishy washy, a bit feeble in the 'raaaaaahhhhh' department, I'm a Harris hawk for goodness sake, I'm dangerous, a hunter I should command fear and respect from all that cross my path".

"Oooh get her! She's been watching ' *Game of Thrones'* again," Syd chortled to Babs.

"Why don't you just belt up you annoying little blue arsed cockolorums. If there's any bitching to be done around here then it's my prerogative!"

"If you're pausing for me to argue you'll be waiting a long time." That was intended to be more under my breath than it actually was. From the moment Sasa had arrived she'd been, shall we say, a little on the militant side, somewhat hostile and always ready for a fight. In the early days she couldn't even go into the mews with the other birds as she was too disruptive. She had mellowed a little.

Sasa looked pretty chuffed with the remark and it didn't go unnoticed with kookaburras.

"Look at her, talk about smugness! You're so clever aren't you Sha'? So bloody smart you dived into a bush and broke your wing!" Sydney was in for the long haul on this one, he'd stuck the knife and now twisted it with precision.

"Just leave the sarcasm and insults to pro's like me. Why don't you find some traffic to play in?" Sha' looked at her feet, a sure sign she was becoming annoyed.

"You'll be so sorry when I learn how to breathe fire!" Bouncing from perch to perch Sydney was starting to enjoy this rapid exchange, he liked a good argument.

"Come on you two, forgive and forget there's no need for all this silliness."

"Forgive and forget? I'm neither Jesus nor do I have Alzheimer's!" Sasa spat out in reply while her eyes bored into Syd's. "Why don't you put the 'fookaburras' enclosure somewhere else and then I wouldn't have to listen to their inane ramblings?"

"Enough Sasa!" I tried to bring the situation under control.

"You daft old bat! Our place is a block built house with a bedroom, two doors, a roof and a huge window, then there's our patio. What are they going to do, take it all apart and put it somewhere else?" By now Syd was howling with laughter, his words faltering as he tried to compose himself. "Whereas you......You sit on................A log. DUH!!!!" Added Babs, keen to get a few words in edgeways.

"Why should I move? I was here first."

"Logistics? A week to move our place, one minute to move your stump. It doesn't take a bloody genius to work it out, mind you your head is only the size of a gobstopper so I doubt that you have the capacity to conjure up much inside it."

"Get me outta' here!" Sasa roared towards me. It was probably the best idea as neither of them were going to back down today and the decibels of a hawk and kookaburra having a fallout is almost off the scale. Sasa was moved to the other side of the garden where Sessi the Alaska Snowy Owl was busy trying to clean his enormous monster feet.

"Oh God, I do NOT want to be next to him! One I can't understand him because he's German and two he talks absolute claptrap without taking a breath." One could say with absolute conviction that no matter where Sasa was put in the garden it would be wrong.

"Kood morning Zaza, it's loffely to haffe zome combany for ein change". Always, polite Sessi stopped admiring his feet and positioned himself to face Sasa.

"What did he say?" Sasa asked, simply trying to prove her aforementioned point. I ignored her, as I turned to walk away the last thing I heard was Sessi starting one of his unusual stories.

"Zere vas ein owvl called Efferard Huko Sdienz und he almost dezerffed it".

Harris's hawks have very low and harsh vocals. They use vocals when with their family, but when their family is hunting together, they choose to use gestures to communicate so that they don't scare away the prey. Biologists believe that they use their tail, more specifically the white terminal bands on their tail, to send out silent signals.

These birds are one of only two known raptor species that hunt as a group. This cooperative hunting style works much like those of mammals, where some members of the group flush out the prey and chase it towards the other hunters in the group. Harris' hawks have excellent vision, possibly 8 times greater than human vision.

The species often performs the art of 'back standing' where literally they stand on each other's backs. Whether to get a better view of the surrounding area or create shade with their wings for those underneath. It's not really known by anyone apart from the birds themselves, they must know why they do it.

Meerkat Law
1. If I like it, it's mine.
2. If it's in my mouth, it's mine.
3. If I had some a little while ago, it's still mine.
4. If I can take it from you, it's mine.
5. If it looks like mine, it's mine.
6. If it's mine it must never be yours.
7. If I saw it first, it's mine.
8. If you have something and put it down, it's mine.

9. If I chew something up, all the pieces are mine.

10. If it's broken, it's yours.
 If you can't be bright at least be ambiguous.

Little Ella is the baby of the family, hatched in 2019 she was, and remains a very chilled girl. It's a bit like living with Phoebe from 'Friends'.

Owls normally have quite an amazing memory for people and places but Ella appears to always be one step behind the rest, she's by no means simple, just in league with the fairies most days. She doesn't seem to have the ability to remember inanimate objects like the bale of sawdust that's kept near the door to the mews, that always makes her jump or her water bowl that has the capability of suddenly lurking from the shadows to spook her.

"Are you coming out little one?" I opened the door to Ella's enclosure fully expecting her to dive into her owl box which she'd normally do if she wasn't ready to go in the garden, all the birds always have the choice if they don't feel like going out.

"Is it hot or cold?" She asked, blinking her enormous eyes very slowly like a Disney character.

"It's neither hot nor cold, sort of tepid really. Everyone else is out but it's up to you," I replied, gathering her jesses.

"Is Matty out? And Molly? What about Sessi and Sasa are they all out?"

"Yep, all out, even Phillip Schofield's out, " I couldn't help myself but it fell on deaf ears."So how about it, in or out?"

"Out would be nice, can I go by the door?" Ella always went in the same basket on the wall, all the smaller owls love sitting in their linen baskets which provide shelter and shade but as they're made from woven plastic they can also see what's going on through the little gaps - Owls are very inquisitive and need to know exactly what's happening, as it happens. Not that anything ever happens but just in case it does they'd hate to miss it.

"Yes, of course you can," with that she jumped onto my gloved hand to be taken out into the garden and her awaiting basket, in plain sight of the door.

I tied her off once she was settled in her hideaway. All the owls have long, thin leashes for their own safety. You can't have two species free flying at the same time otherwise they could all end up eating each other, think Russian dolls.

"The door, where does it go?" Ella asked.

"I'm pretty sure it stays where it is," I replied.

"You know what I mean, I know it's not a *'Harry Potter'* door that moves around when it feels like it, what's behind it?" It was sometimes quite shocking to realise just how much television the owls watched when we weren't looking or in Molly's case Internet shopping.

"That door?" I teased.

"Yes! That door, the one with the glass in." If an owl could roll its eyes (which they can't as they're fixed in their sockets) then Ella would have done so.

"It's the doorway into another dimension actually. If you urgently need to visit another country like Ga Ga does all too often (note to self I need to have words with her before too long) then you simply go in, closing the door behind you of course and then tell the gecko which is always suckered to the wall which destination you require. Don't forget to tell him/her that it's a return ticket you need, otherwise you'd be stuck wherever you fancied visiting for eternity".

Ella sat in silence leaning forward a little, ready for the next instalment, her eyes even larger than normal.

"Matty went to Norway last week, didn't you Matty?" I shouted across to the snoozing Eagle owl who could always be relied upon to answer any question.

"Yep" came her standard reply unless it was 'nahh' which was her other choice when not at all engaged with the subject under discussion.

"She popped over to Norway to fly across the fjords, it was her birthday treat. I think she probably just sat in an enormous Pine tree rather than expending any effort at all by flying but that's what she said when she got back." I was starting to wonder just how long I could keep this up.

"How do you think Syd the Kookaburra got here? I added, trying to keep a straight face.

"I thought he came from Cadiz," replied Ella. Of course she was correct as Syd had come from a vet there who had confiscated him from his previous owner - Another story.

"No, we only say that to people because if everyone knew there was a travel portal behind the door they'd want to use it and we'd have thousands of people wandering backwards and forwards through the garden with their luggage and a host of screaming children in tow. Sydney forgot to ask for a return ticket when he left Australia but when he arrived he liked being here so much he stayed."

"Wow! I never knew any of this." Little Ella looked quite aghast at what she'd just heard. "All of that goes on behind that door".

Now all we have to do is remember to not open the door while Ella is in the garden otherwise she'll realise it's just the boiler room, littered with garden tools and pots of paint. There is a large fat gecko suckered to the wall though.

Most know but for those who don't, we get many rescues in but Mungo & Midge have been the smallest so far.

We'd planted a field of potatoes and come Spring it was time to start lifting them, which was when their nest was accidently excavated. Luckily they were spotted and brought immediately into the house.

They were no larger than a pinto bean, bald and pink. As the weather was still on the cool side my immediate thoughts were about how to keep them warm enough and safe from the cats. There are few places here that the felines cannot access in order to sleep soundly, normally on some form of paperwork or items deemed vaguely important. However there was one place, a glass fronted dresser.

An elaborate box consisting of a pocket from an old pair of fluffy PJ's (why they need pockets goodness only knows), a rather plush towel that had never performed its only duty sufficiently enough for my liking and kitchen roll for the pee and poo collection. The box was then placed upon a hot water bottle wrapped in a towel and both were lowered into another box for stability. They had a mouse nursery.

Now, this all worked a treat for two hours at a time and then the water bottle would gradually get cooler so I would have to get up each night at intervals to take a layer of towelling away or boil a kettle so as to maintain the perfect temperature throughout the night.

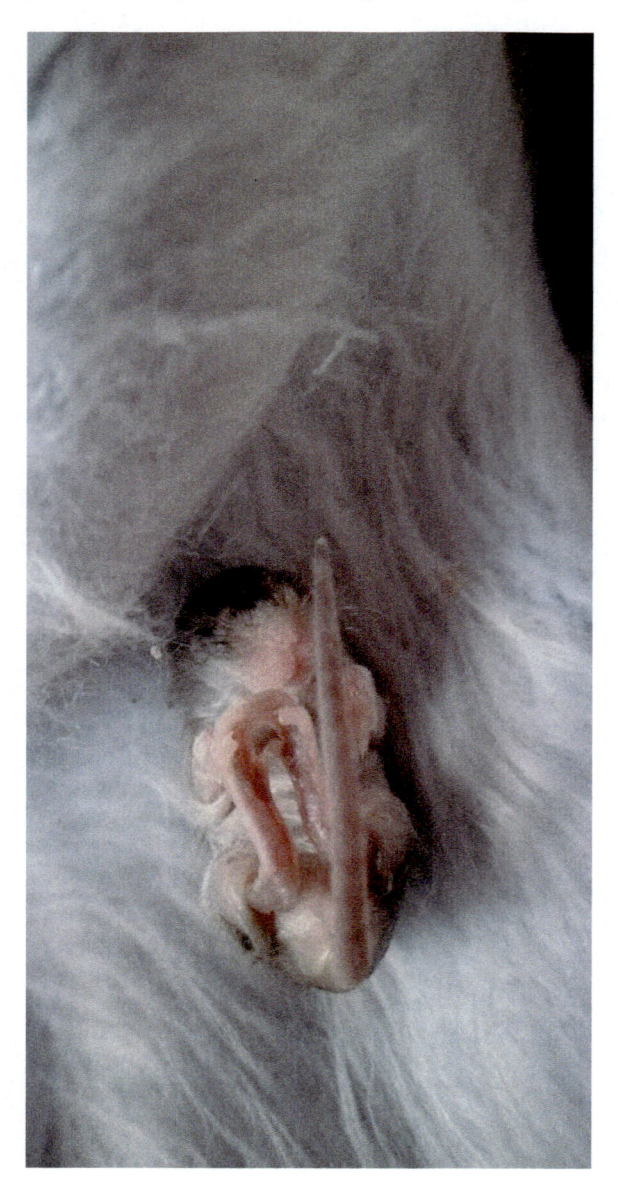

Mungo & Midge thrived on a weak mix of kitten formula and were soon eating solids (thank goodness) but that in itself brought another change in the heating arrangements.

As they were starting to move around I found they'd moved away from the nest overnight and one morning they were really quite cool so I had to rethink the hot water bottle idea. A quick re- make of their nest, a new larger box, this time with a powder blue angora scarf and candles. They were placed on one side of the dresser with a lid on their box and various candles in safety lamps and large jars of hot water filled the dresser to keep the ambient temperature nice and toasty. So for another week or so they lived quite happily, learning to eat grain in their climate controlled pad.

The day came for them to go into the wild and it was a lovely warm Summer's morning. I popped some grain, the last of the scarf and the little wicker basket into the car and then went to get Mungo & Midge from the dresser. We were all set and I had the perfect place in mind to put them, the ruined mill house next door. It was not far from where they'd been dug up, it was dry and enormous so lots of space to run around, hide and explore. To access outside there was a gap under the door just large enough for mice so there were bound to be other mice in the building.

All was going according to plan until I reached the mill and went to get Mungo & Midge out of the box, only one mouse!

I sped back home and when I reached the dresser there was the other standing up on its hind legs looking out of the glass front like an abandoned child. Needless to say they were both released together into the old mill where hopefully they used it wisely as their first home before going out into the big wide world.

When looking for food, these rodents often collect and disperse leaves, twigs and other visually conspicuous objects that serve as landmarks as they explore the area.

In spite of its small size and a very tiny stomach, this rodent has a big appetite, eating as often as 15 - 20 times per day. This is the reason why mice tend to live near food sources.

Field mice are excellent climbers. They are known to use abandoned bird nests, located high in trees and providing them with secluded places, where they can enjoy berries and other types of food that they have cached. They rarely move and usually live in the same area. Wood mice are known to take night trips of quarter of a mile (400m).

Matty has underlying issues, as she's still a youngster everything that's new can't be trusted whether it's a cushion or a Carpenter Bee. If she hasn't seen it before then she's scared of it.

"What on earth are you doing under there Matty?" I'd only put her in the garden ten minutes earlier so I was more than surprised to see that she was under the bar area, which has never been used as a bar but seemed such a good idea at the time.

"There's a wotsit out there looking at me."

"A puffed cheesy snack is watching you?" I asked. One had to smile but not in a flashy toothed way which would upset this great big mound of Eagle Owl.

"What? No, don't be ridiculous! It's a thing, it's got eyes and it's staring at me." Shuffling from foot to foot Matty was certainly agitated about whatever it was she'd spotted.

"Where is it?"

"On the wall over there, it just keeps peering at me."

I looked across to where Matty had indicated and saw nothing intimidating at all, no dogs, cats, birds or anything else that could frighten a major predator.

"I can't see anything big girl, why don't you come out from under the bar and show me."

Feeling a little braver she hopped up onto her tree stump so that she had a better view.

"There, there it is. Look!"

Following her eye line I eventually worked out what it was she was so upset about. I'd left my pink gardening gloves on the wall with the fingers pointing towards where Matty was sitting and I'd put a pair of secateurs on top so from her position the ends of the handles looked like eyes and this horrible creature had an anemone styled tongue. I could certainly see why she'd freaked out.

I walked over and picked up the creature from hell to show Matty that it's components were totally harmless.

"Are you OK now?"

"Yep." She was back to her normal monosyllabic self.

"Why did you take the glove with you, did it make you feel safer?"

"No, that's where my food comes from. I thought that if I had to stay under the bar all day at least I wouldn't go hungry."

All of the owls think that food magically appears on falconry gloves, that's why they love to fly to a gloved hand. Or indeed fly over the top of it to see what's on offer first, one of Molly's tricks as if she feels the quantity of sustenance is not up to her very exacting standard she'll help herself from the food dish and ignore the glove.

All owlets have to be taught various things and bathing is one of them. Although hard wired to have a bath once they're in water, they need to experience what water is first of all.

Owls are scrupulously clean birds and if they're not sleeping they're cleaning, one way or another. Flying cats when all is said and done.

We introduce all the owlets to a water bowl at about three weeks old, if at all possible out in the garden when it's lovely and sunny so that they dry off rapidly, nothing worse than a miserably wet owl.

Mystic of course was no exception, the time came one early afternoon to prepare the tepid bath for her first experience of water. A kettle was boiled and tipped into the awaiting brand new bowl (they all have their own) and ample cool water was added to make it a perfect temperature for her.

Very slowly I lowered Mystic down into the water on my hand so that it wouldn't be a shock in any way.

She went ballistic, we'd never seen an owl act in such a way. Of course we took her out of the bowl immediately and calmed her down. Thinking that it was just a one off reaction the following week we tried it again, she was a little better but it was a short lived exercise. Week after week we went through the same procedure but there was little improvement.

Although she'd stand in the water she made no attempt at all to bathe, instead she'd just scowl until lifted back out.

I looked on the Internet about Northern White Faced Owls but there was nothing said about them disliking water, there was actually not a scrap of information on them bathing at all.

OK so we have a water loathing dirty owl, we need to come up with a solution to suit all involved. Having kept chickens for years, I wondered whether Mystic would prefer to take a dust bath. I bought a cat litter tray and filled it with fine dry earth and popped it into her night cage.

Sure enough she dived into it and bathed up a storm, clouds of earth puffed up around her like an explosion. She is the only species of owl that drinks water and bathes in dust, we know that now.

So it must have seemed bizarre to her that we kept putting her in her drinking water. The look on her face in the photo is hilarious. She has subsequently taught Pippin the Little Owl to bathe in dust too as they used to live next door to each other, now Pippin has been released we often wonder if she's been caught on camera having a dust bath in the wild.

There is nothing about falconry that can only be performed by a man, it is equally enjoyable and as frustrating to both sexes however there's one thing you should always bare in mind when handling a white bird. Don't wear makeup, that goes for fella's too!

As Sesi the Alaska owls main handler I learnt within a couple of days that I couldn't wear a scrap of make up because come what may he'd get covered in it. Very much like cooking with chocolate goodness knows where it all comes from but within seconds you're plastered with the bloody stuff.

"Sesi, you're going pink".

"Nein I zink vu'll find I am zee schtandard regulazion vite vith ein little black ere und zere".

Hatched and raised for four years in Germany Sesi's accent is a little strong but he's learning everyday. Unfortunately like Mystic he's not keen on water so bathing is a bit of a chore and as we don't have an ample supply of snow available to him, he hasn't much of a choice in the matter.

"You've got rouge on the top of your head so you're going to have a quick wash seeing as your personal hygiene routine is somewhat lackadaisical to say the least".

"One, I don't know vat vu mean py rouge und tvo how did it get on mein head?" Sesi replied looking quite defiant, well as much as the big softy can.

"It's come off my face, it's makeup and now it's not on me but on you. We need to remove it because quite frankly it doesn't do anything for you at all. I'm not sure it does anything for me either but one must try to look reasonably presentable and not scare you lot with my pallid Winter complexion". I headed off to get a bowl of water so he could take a bath.

"Vats zat?" Sesi asked as I put the large bowl of water in front of him.

"It's a fedora wearing racoon juggling with bananas". I replied flippantly knowing that I was going to have a battle on my hands.

"Nein it's not, it's ein povl of vater".

"Well now that's been established, would you kindly get in the bowl and have a bath?".

"I vill pathe lader ven nopody is looking, any vay it's too........" He trailed off knowing that whichever temperature he was about to complain about would be pointless as the bath water was always tepid.

"When nobody is looking? It's not as if you take your feathers off, why the shyness? I had to smile.

"I brefer to vasch vizout ein hautience, zat's all".

"You prefer to make out that you've had a bath overnight when you're in the mews, that's the truth of the matter. Well I'm afraid I'm going to have to wash the makeup from your head whether you like it or not and I suspect you won't". With that I popped a cloth in the water, squeezed out the residue and started to clean Sesi's feathers on top of his head.

Luckily the makeup came off quite easily, feeling somewhat ripped off by how light weight it was in comparison with how much the 'Stay-Put-Super-Density-Waterproof' rouge had cost me but I was placated given the situation.

"There, all done!" I announced taking one final look over his plumage to see there were no other areas that needed cleaning. With one last flourish of the cloth I gave his tail a quick once over just to remove some food that he'd flicked on to it.

"I most cerdainly did not haffe any of your make up on mein tail, I am alvays most careful not to get mein bosderior near to your face".

And for that Sesi, we can be most grateful.

"Have you heard the Meerkats have managed to get on the Internet?"
"No."
"Yeah, according to Greta they've somehow cobbled a system together and when Peachey got out the other day she moved the dish thing a bit so that they get a bounced signal down into their enclosure."
"Who's Greta?"
"You know our LGBTQ+ poultry representative, he started off as a she and turned into a he, the big grey one, always smells nice."
"Oh yeah, he's lovely, always immaculate."
"That's the one."
"So have they got a computer in there too?"
"No, a mobile phone. Apparently they got it from Snatchy the shepherd's dog, somebody dropped it in the valley and you know what he's like!"
"Oh he's always been a light pawed that one, wouldn't trust him as far as I could throw him".
"Have you thrown a dog then?"
"In my younger days. So what are the Meerkats doing, watching films and stuff?".
"Greta says that Peachey is rinsing *Meerkat Manor,* watching them back to back and pointing out all the things that Meerkats wouldn't do. According to her it's all staged, when they finish filming they all go off to a hotel somewhere and have cocktails."
"What on earth do they do with cock tails?"

"No cocktails dear, they're drinks."

"Oh right, I had images of all those little Meerkats running around with feathers on their heads. So what's Florian doing while madam is watching TV?"

"You know him, he's his fathers son for sure. He could be improving his education or taking up a hobby but as always he's sat in the sun."

"Scratching his wotnots?"

"Of course, says that he has to keep checking they're still there as the dogs and cats have reported theirs vanished after a long sleep."

"What are you two up to? Pixie, play nicely with Ella won't you."

"She won't get out of my box."

"No, you won't get out of my box, I was here first."

"Share the box between you, I don't want to hear any arguments".

"Right she's gone into the kitchen, what was I saying?"

"Something about toys."

"That was it!. Why is it that you lot, cats in general not the whole of the Maine Coon species, have got loads of toys? You've got brightly coloured mice with feathery tails, I don't know what that's all about but hey they are cute. Balls with bells, plush fish that you throw around although I'm not keen on fish. What have we got? Nothing! Not a toy in sight, bugga all".

"That's true", Pixie mused. "You can play with my toys if you want, she said we've got to share."

"Thanks Pix' but I want my own things with less cat spit on them if you don't mind."

"No, that's a fair point well made. So what sort of toys do you want?"

"Snakes & Ladders for sure, Bat a Rat, Sneaky Snacky Squirrel and Chickapig to start with."

"Wow, you've really thought about this haven't you? So are you going to ask her for them in a minute?"

"Well I thought it would be better coming from you, you're older and have a way with words that I just haven't got around to yet. Would you mind?"

"No, I'll go into the kitchen now. Hang on there for a minute."

With that Pixie sauntered into the kitchen and sat patiently by my feet as I was doing the washing up.

"Can I have a moment?"

"Well as you asked so nicely Pixie of course you can, what's on your mind?"

"Poor Ella hasn't any toys to play with, the cats and I have loads but she doesn't want them. I did offer to share like you said we should."

"Well you're a very good girl Pix' and Ella's a little too young to have any toys at the moment."

"But I had toys when I was young."

"That's true but cats don't try and swallow their toys whole."

"And Maine Coon's? Remember I'm not an ordinary cat."

"Or Maine Coon's, how could I forget. I think you'll find that Ella has her eyes on any toys that involve animals or birds. You've seen the adverts on TV for companies that deliver food haven't you? Where the end sequence is somebody opening a pizza box or fried chicken bucket, well I think that's what Ella's hoping for. A box of snakes, rats or squirrels etc."

"Has she mentioned it before then?"

"Just a few times, daily."

"I feel such a fool, she conned me into asking you."

"She's not called 'Little H'Ella' for nothing you know."

"Good morning Molly, are you coming outside?"

"No, I'm busy."

"Doing what? It's a lovely day, not too cold or windy. You should really get some fresh air and have a good fly around the garden".

"I did that yesterday. I'd prefer to stay in the mews if it's all the same to you, I've got to a really good bit in my book and you know how it is, I want to see how it ends."

"I do indeed, what are you reading Hemmingway again?"

"No, the King James version of *The Bible.*"

"Gosh, that's a big read!"

"I'm just at the *Shrek* bit, it's not as funny as the films but it's OK".

"I didn't know there was a parable involving Shrek, you live and learn hey?"

"Well there's been no mention of *Shrek* so far but the talking donkey is in it, plus there's an angel with a sword. It's all quite exciting. I get the impression that this God chap was just about at the end of his tether with folk. He keeps warning everyone not to do things and they simply ignore him all the time or they are constantly moaning. Then he has to bring out the 'big guns' so to speak and hammer the advice home."

"Mmm I tend to agree with you, I always thought that the fish parable was funny."

"Oh yeah, serves them right for bitching about having to eat banana."

"Manna."

"Whatever. I wonder if fish did come down through their noses."

"What would you write if you could add a parable?"

"That's easy. One should bathe at least once a day."

"I think 'cleanliness is next to godliness' is already featured Molly."

"No, in my version it would be cleanliness is next to compliments. Everyone always remarks on how beautifully white my chest is, that doesn't happen by accident you know, I spend hours preening each day."

"Ooh Mol' I think you would be committing one of the deadly sins, namely pride."

"Me and the rest of the mews then! Greedy Sesi, the wrath of Matty, Darcy the glutton, lusty Sasa, slothy Silas and envious Ella among the lot of us we've got it covered."

"Yep, pretty much sewn up. I'll leave you to it then, enjoy your reading matter and I'll see you later."

"For the 'last supper' perhaps?"

"Smarty pants!"

"Do you know why we're waiting?"

"No, I'm not sure. Are we waiting?"

"Well, we're standing still in silence so I could only think that we're waiting for something."

"You don't think we're asleep do you?"

"No, I'm fairly sure we have to sit down and close our eyes for that."

"Yeah, true. Maybe we're waiting for food."

"I don't think so, food usually comes in a glass bowl with tweezers and we're in a plastic bowl and I can't see the tweezers."

"You don't think we're the food do you?"

"No, don't be stupid. If anything, I think we're waiting for a bath."

"I'm not keen on those, they seem to happen at least every twenty years."

"We're only three weeks old, how can they happen every twenty years?"

"I'm a kestrel chick. I have no notion of time or space if I'm honest. Einstein introduced the concept of a fourth dimension time, that meant that space and time were inextricably linked. The general theory of relativity suggests that space-time expands and contracts depending on the momentum and mass of nearby matter."

"I heard all of the words but I didn't understand any of it."

"Me neither, don't know where that all came from."

"Perhaps you've lived another life where you understood stuff like that, a scientist or professor of things. Maybe you were a genius and now you've been born again, you'll be the cleverest kestrel in the world."

"What, reinstallation ?"

"Yeah, something like that. I'd just like to take back most of what I've just said."

In mediaeval times the Kestrel would have been the hunting bird of a knave, reflecting just how far down the social scale he was.

A king or high nobility would choose a Gyrfalcon, the largest of the falcon family and no doubt costly as their natural habitat was Arctic coasts, tundra and the islands of northern North America and the Eurosiberian region.

Eggs or chicks would be taken from nests and sold to the highest bidder across the world whereas Kestrels would have been prevalent throughout Europe and America so far easier to obtain. Fortunately it is now illegal to take chicks from the wild.

'As darkness cast it's veil, Isaac began to feel almost vulnerable as he struggled to make his way through the undergrowth, he was sure he was being watched. What had been a welcome gentle breeze in the latter part of the afternoon was now chilling him, adding to his general feeling of urgency to find somewhere safe to rest. A primal need was taking over.

From the corner of his eye he saw a willowy figure standing on a small hillock, he couldn't make out any features from such a distance but he knew it was a woman. He headed toward her hoping that she knew of a hamlet or village close by, anywhere he could rest.

The vision became clearer. It was a girl in her teenage years, perhaps a little older. Hair waist length russet coloured hair plaited to one side. She was dressed in a green velvet cloak with the hood down. She stood motionless but didn't appear to be concerned by his presence.

"Please don't be scared, I will not bring you any harm," his voice slightly raised above the evening birdsong in the trees.

"I have no fear of you Sir," she beckoned Isaac towards her. "My name is Brenna, I'm from the house of Saint Dogild".

She was indeed a beauty with a fair complexion and dark, almost magical green eyes of a colour he'd never seen before. He felt relieved to have found another soul to guide him but what was this young, somewhat beguiling girl doing in the woods after dark?

Brenna noticed the stranger's shirt and skin, torn from the brambles and thickets, droplets of blood fell to the ground leaving a trail for those seeking sustenance.

"You alright Mystic?"

"Yes, yes I'm fine."

"You look a little startled, that's all."

"I was just making up a story but it all started to go a bit scary."

"Oh dear. How about you choose something else, what about a safari setting, you originate from Sudan after all"

"Mmm, I could try I suppose".

'Diana stood up to leave the warm glow of the campfire, it had been a long and dusty day. All she wanted now was a cool wash and her sleeping bag, maybe she'd read her book for a while until sleep took over.

She mused over the odd conversation she'd had with her coworker earlier that day, they'd been a team for so many years yet the look in his eyes was different somehow, softer and playful. They'd been discussing the possibility of pitching camp above a small watering hole, far enough away so as not to disturb the wildlife seeking a drink but close enough to watch as they did.

"That's a wonderful idea Ben, if we set the trail cam' out by the waters edge we should get some great footage." Both of them had worked on wildlife documentaries for some time, Diana put together the route and Ben collated all of the camera sets so that the production team had a script to work to when they arrived.

"Yeah, I think it could work quite well" Ben then paused. "Plus it'll be a great place to watch the sun go down together, maybe we can enjoy a beer or two while we relax."

"Good idea," replied Diana, not really tuning into his suggestion fully.

The plan was only partly put into action, the trail camera was set up. The location and sunset were perfect but Ben had spent most of the evening on the phone dealing with work schedules so Diana had enjoyed a tepid beer while watching antelope drinking from the oasis. Hundreds of tiny mice scuttled around the water's edge taking their fill, not concerned about plodding hooves they stopped and cleaned themselves, their whiskers...................

"Oh bugga!"

"What's up now Mystic, how's that story going?"

She quickly ran through it for me with perfect eloquence which White Faced owls tend to possess.

"Both stories are very good 'Myst, with quite a bit of romantic content creeping in. You're not getting broody are you?" I asked, smiling at her. Spring is an odd time for all of the young ladies in the mews after all.

"Don't be so daft, I'm not broody. Isaac with his arms like a bloody steak and then Diana watching a horde of mice, it's nothing to do with romance. I'm famished!"

"Lunch it is then, are you going to do any more of your stories afterwards?"

"Ooh no, I'll need a little sleep until this evening. I don't want to overdo it and end up with writer's block".

With that Mystic downed her lunch in one and within a minute was fluffed up and fast off, nice work if you can get it.

The colour of an owl's eyes is a good indicator of when they hunt.

If the owl has black eyes this means they can capture prey in total darkness with their incredible sense of hearing.

There's a chance you might see one of these owls in daylight on a cloudy day, but these sightings are treasured moments.

Owls with orange eyes are crepuscular, meaning they're active during low light periods such as dusk and dawn.

Owls with yellow eyes are diurnal and prefer to hunt during the daytime.

"You look exceedingly cute Pippin."

"Yeah, I know. Any sort of feather works on a bird, even if they don't belong, they just give us a certain ``je ne sais quoi."

"You've got a look of Audrey Hepburn about you."

"I don't know who that is so I'll just agree, it's obviously somebody ancient so that's your department."

"Cheers for that Pip' it's always nice to be reminded that the years are now hammering past like stanchions on the motorway."

"I think you should make us up, or me to be blunt, a dressing up box."

"If it will keep you entertained when it's cold and rainy, I'll happily do that but you'll have to share it with Molly. You know how much she loves getting glam'd up."

"I suppose, she's bigger so we won't really be wearing the same outfits anyway."

"Hang on a minute, we were talking about feathers and now we've drifted over to 'outfits' which sounds like a little more work. What exactly are you thinking of?"

"Feathers, yes. Brightly coloured boa's, you could cut them in half and we'd have one each so we wouldn't have to share those."

"I could cut them into ten and then you'd all have one each, have you seen the length of a feather boa?"

Pippin dismissed this comment with a slightly withering look in my direction.

"Silk scarves are good too, same idea but they'd need hemming where you cut them in half, we don't want any bits hanging off them. Then we could have proper little clothes to dress up in, I'd like a pair of jeans with pockets, I've always thought pockets would be really useful. Dungarees would be even better because there's five pockets, I'd put all sorts of things in five of them."

"Tiny weeny jeans, your size?"

"With pockets and a zip. Oh and a belt too, they don't look cool unless you've got a belt on them, I don't want empty loop syndrome."

"Oh heaven help us, that would be a travesty!"

"You won't have to make any jeans for Molly, her legs go up to her chin so she'd look ridiculous. Mind you it would be worth the laugh, yeah do her some too."

"That's a bit cruel Pippin, she's just designed differently to you. Some would say that Little owls are dumpy in comparison to Barn owls."

"Make those jeans skinny then, that way my legs will look longer. Oh and I'll need a range of formal and evening wear as well. Fairly classic that I can dress up or dress down. Sequins would be nice."

"Sequins on you would be like wearing shiny tea plates, I don't think they're a good idea".

"That's true I hadn't considered the scale, how about metallic material? Golds and silvers? I rather like a shimmer."

"I'm now thinking of the 70's disco scene, that's really not a good look."

"You know, I'm beginning to think that you may not be up to the job."

"I think you're absolutely correct Pip', I don't think creating owl haute couture is really my forte. I'm better at preparing endless amounts of food and cleaning the mews, I'm quite adept at any tasks that require me to scrabble around on the floor or get filthy, if the two can be combined I'm in veritable heaven."

"Can you at least get some feathers? That would be a start and then I can get Molly to look on the Internet for more options, she's got the new Iphone 13 mini version you know".

"Has she indeed, where did that come from? I hope to goodness she's not used my debit card again. It was somewhat of a surprise to find a transaction for a crystal encrusted tiara, I don't have a lot of use for one of those."

"Especially with your hair!"

"Cheers Pippin! Nice of you to point that out."

"You alright ladies, enjoying the evening sun?"

"I'd like to report that it is indeed lovely and relaxing, however Noné's snoring like a pig!"

"Nudge her, she'll soon stop."

"I'm not nudging her, you do it!"

"Can't you see I'm carrying a washing basket? I've literally got my hands full."

"If I wake her she'll bat me, she won't bat you."

"Matty, you're a 10kg plus European Eagle owl and you're frightened of a cat that's giving Methuselah a run for his money?"

"Yeah, too right! She packs a punch, it's all that sleeping. I reckon the more she sleeps the stronger she becomes and I've put up with this snoring for hours, she's going to dish it out like Tyson if you wake her."

"OK. I'll sort it. Noné! NONÉ! Wake up, you're snoring!"

"Hmmmm……….I wasn't snoring, just resting my eyes. Who said I was snoring?"

"I heard you as I was walking past, poor Matty's been sitting there with you sounding like a chainsaw."

"That was purring, I was purring at Matty to send her to sleep. It's a very relaxing sound, it's what mothers do to send their kittens off to the land of nod."

"Purring? Bloody purgatory more like! That racket wouldn't send anything off to sleep, you can snore both ways. Not just breathing in but out too, double the noise! I never realised you could fit so much air into one cat, with lungs like yours you must be able to blow up hot water bottles!"

"I've never tried that, sounds quite exhausting though. In all honesty I can't see the point in blowing those up, what would you do with them then?"

"I think perhaps Matty could think of something useful to do with it!"

"Hey Houdi' how you doin'?"
"Fine."
"A fella of few words aren't you?"
"Yep."
"Indulge me for a moment, how can you get to the top of a 2m ladder when you can't fly?"

"Oh, you noticed that?"

"So much so little mate I've now got a photo to prove it."

Houdini (so aptly named) came in a few years ago from Malaga with a damaged scapula, basically his shoulder joint dislocates in full flight so he couldn't be released again. However he's got a special job which is as a companion to any Little owl fosters, he shows them the ropes and keeps them company until they're released again. Although very shy when it comes to people, he does love playing the head bobbing game from a distance.

"I pole vaulted."

"Really?"

"Yep, off that bamboo cane."

"That's impressive! So you're saying you ran along, scooped up the end of the bamboo in your wing tips, hurled yourself skywards and then leapt on to the top of the ladder?"

"More or less."

"Wow, that's incredible! Why didn't you walk up the thick piece of rope that goes from floor to ceiling and then jump down onto the ladder?"

"I thought about it but where's the challenge in that?"

"True."

"He did walk up the rope," a little voice piped up from the corner of the aviary.

"No I didn't Lucy! And anyway you can't see anything, you're as blind as a door knob so how would you know?"

"I could hear you puffing all the way up, if you'd pole vaulted any owl worth it's feathers would have employed a 'wooooooo' once leaving the pole. Instead I heard heavy talons against aluminium as you jumped down from the rope."

"Oh great, why do I have to share the aviary with Miss. Bloody - Marple over there?"

"Cos' she keeps it real little mate."

"Pippin, how do you plead? Guilty or not guilty?"

"Oh you think you're so funny don't you? How do you expect me to look when I've just been misted with water, that was the last thing I was expecting."

In the heat of the Summer there are misting systems here that keep the birds cool while they're outside in the morning, it also gives them an ideal opportunity to bathe as well, especially for the boys who aren't that keen.

"Prisoner Pippity Pippin, return to your cell."

"Oh give it a rest."

"Don't be such a spoil sport, what would be your crime?"

"Killing anyone that turns on the misters when I'm dozing in my basket."

All the owls apart from Sesi and Matty, have small plastic linen baskets attached to the walls in the garden which give them shade but they can look through the small holes to keep abreast of anything interesting going on. The world hasn't come up with a basket large enough to fit the big ones in.

"You could swoop into a museum and steal a precious artefact, have it away in your talons and then swoop back out again."

"So for arguments sake I steal a Fabergé egg, I can't eat it can I? It's not as if my social circle contains billionaires who would want to buy it, mind you I reckon Molly's sitting on a few bob and she loves anything garish."

"OK, fair point well made. What would you choose to pinch then? If indeed you went down the route of theft to warrant your prison sentence."

"A fast car, Audi, Merc' BMW. Anything along those lines. A new one of course, nothing clapped out."

"I think you may struggle to nick a car unless you've got telescopic legs and opposable thumb feathers. You're only 22cm tall, you'd have a job to reach the pedals."

Pippin looked at me with eyes full of disdain.

"I'd be the mastermind behind it, choosing the targets and deciding when and where they'd be taken. They'd have to be hidden somewhere, number plates changed, chassis numbers removed and then of course buyers would need to be found. I'd get them out of the country as soon as possible, that way the cops would have a harder job tracking them down."

"Aah I see, I did wonder how you'd be able to drive them away without being able to see through the windscreen. So who would you choose to do your dirty work?"

"I'd go for the least likely candidate, that way nobody would imagine what was going on. Somebody quiet, a bit on the daft side but could drive."

"That sounds reasonable enough, when are you going to start your life of crime Pip'?"

"Depends on if you want the job".

"I do not appreciate being bundled up in an old towel and carted through the house."

"Well I'm sorry but you can't live in my bedroom and a dogs towel was the only thing I had to hand, it had been washed you know."

"Not sufficiently in my opinion!"

"What were you doing in the house anyway? You're hardly pocket sized like the geckos, what are you 80cm long?"

"If I sit straight I'm 83cm in length if you don't mind. It was hardly my choice to be in your bedroom, I didn't wake up one day and think to myself 'Oh I know what I'll do, move into what looks like Miss.Havisham's boudoir for a spell, that'll be nice' did I?"

"I don't know what you Ocellated lizards think, so how did you end up in there anyway?"

"Your ghastly hunter/killer cat! Blasted thing tracked me through the esparto grass, I couldn't shake her off so when she leapt at me I reciprocated and somehow clamped my mouth shut on her collar. That spooked her so she ran. It was like riding a bucking bronco, I was in the air then hurtling across the ground and then boom! She shot through the window and I was catapulted onto the big squishy thing."

"My bed?"

"No idea what it was but there was a lot of it in the middle of the room and appeared to be covered in clothes. Are you underprivileged, do you have to sleep under coats to keep warm? I've heard it's a real thing, you lot put your children to bed under the contents of a wardrobe. Shameful."

"That was clean washing ready to put away, you didn't wee on it did you? And no we don't put kids to bed like that, you're talking about a couple of centuries ago when many families were terribly poor and couldn't afford to heat their houses."

"Of course I didn't 'wee' on it! What d' you think I am, a puppy that piddles everywhere at the meerest sign of attention?!"

"A shirty lizard is what I think you are at the moment. So what did you do then?"

"Had a cup of tea and did a crossword puzzle," I was convinced it rolled its eyes at me at this point.

"I was traumatised after the experience, puffed out and I'd gone pale all over. That's how bad I felt so I went under the covers to hide for a while and gather some strength."

"Ewww you weren't still in my bed later that night were you?"

"Oh good gracious no! What a repugnant thought, no certainly not. By that time I'd found sanctuary under a piece of furniture, and also found a sock incidentally."

"Ooh handy".

"Well more socky to be truthful."

"How long were you hiding in the bedroom then?"

"It seemed like a bloody eternity, I tried to find a way out but the window was too high and I did peek around the door into the hallway but there was just too much noise going on."

"I thought you Lacertilia's had sucky feet and could climb up anything."

"Well done on the Latin, it's a pity you fell at the 'sucky feet' hurdle. We have miniscule hairs on our feet called setae which enable us to climb almost any surface gracefully and often at speed."

"Any surface apart from bedroom walls then? Well that's a blessing in disguise, I'd hate to have one of you fall on me during the night. So you still haven't told me how long you were hiding under the wardrobe."

"I think it was three nights, I couldn't find anything to eat, I was fading fast and all seemed hopeless."

"Did you try and eat a toilet roll in the bathroom?"

"Mmmm yes, not my first choice of sustenance but I was ravenous".

"I thought one of the cats had been scatting it around the floor, mystery solved. Anyway, you're outside now in the sunshine, you've had a bit of raw egg to cheer you up and have lived to tell the tale. You're in the corral garden at the moment so do you want me to put you back into the esparto grass on the hill up the lane?"

"Hold on, I'm rather taken with this area. That esparto is scratchy to the skin and I'm starting to think I'd quite like to stay here, it's sheltered and you could probably do with a bit of garden management. I eat the bugs and you keep out of my way. How does that sound?"

"That's fine with me, don't run at me and snap at my ankles though. It's most off putting. I had that experience in Castril, lovely village but in the countryside it's rife with your sort and they're all angry."

"Oh that's my distant cousins clan probably, they're all a bit like that. Archimedes runs a tight ship so to speak, animals in the campo and humans in the village."

"Do you have a name?"

"Of course I do, it's Squizxiudgiossamentii after my father."

"Gosh! Well……..Um…….Squizii, sorry I'm going to have to abbreviate it as my life is slipping away. Do you mind?"

"No, I quite like it actually."

"That's good, well help yourself to the bugs in the garden and perhaps you'd like to take up residence in the boiler room, it's quite warm during the Winter and nobody ever investigates what's at the back so you could set yourself up a nice little pad."

"I'll give it the once over, I'm not making any promises though. I'm fairly choosy about my accommodation".

And so it was that Squizii did move into the boiler room and has been there ever since, sometimes you can see him sunbathing on a flat stone in the garden but as promised we leave each other alone. He does chase GaGa the cat occasionally who still has nightmares about their initial encounter, it's stopped her catching lizards that's for sure.

The ocellated lizard is the largest lizard in Europe, measuring up to 70 cm in length. The juveniles are insectivores, while adults have an omnivorous diet based on other reptiles, such as small lizards, small birds and small mammals like shrews and mice. Its natural predators are the ladder snake and birds of prey.

They inhabit arid areas, from woodlands and grasslands to vineyards and olive groves where they take refuge in burrows and foliage. Not at all sociable apart from during breeding these lizards prefer to live alone.

"What can you see Pixie?"

" Firewood mainly, I'm sure there's something moving around in there though."

"Like what? Is it a mousey? I love mouseys, say it's a mousey."

"It's a mousey."

"Is it really? Oh fantastic, scoot it out this way I'll catch it for us (me)."

"It's not really, I was just joking. I think it's one of those black beetles with the back legs higher than its front ones, I don't know what they're called."

"I don't like those, they always look a bit menacing as they lurch towards you. Leave it there and we can carry on playing with my blanket."

"If I could only get these fireside tool things out of the way I could really get in there."

"Shall I have a look? I'm smaller, well not as long as you. Mind you you've got big paddy feet to dig around with, you're better equipped than me for furtling in a wood pile."

"I can hear clicking."

"What sort of clicking, like I click?"

"Sort of a clickity clicking."

"Oh that's nailed it then! I bet it's a teeny weeny angry owl and any minute now it will come hurtling out and attack us."

"What like Fuji? Just have a look to see that she's in her cage will you?"

"No it's not Fuji, she's in her box stomping around."

"Well that's good news, she's a monster on a bad day".

"Not much different on a good day to be honest, she was gobbing off at Matty the other day. Frightened the pants off her."

"And those are some pants!"

"You're not wrong. Are we any closer to knowing what's clicking in the woodpile? I can feel lunch coming on and I'm a bit bored just talking to your bottom constantly."

"It's all gone quiet, whatever it was is waiting for us to go away."

"Shall we play with the blanket then? I'll sit on it and you can drag me around the floor."

"Why don't I sit on it? You can pull it with your beak, I don't want to go too fast though."

With that Pixie the Maine Coon plonked herself down on the dishevelled blanket in preparation for lift off and Ella walked straight past her into the kitchen for a spot of lunch. Tawny owlets have a short span of attention but a large window of opportunity for food.

The clicking was from a wind up yellow chick toy, as it wasn't found by the pair of them it was employed again to keep them entertained another half dozen times. The best 90 cents I've ever spent!

"Where have your feet gone Mystic?"
"I'm not sure, I think they're where they should be but I haven't seen them this morning so I'm not answering with complete assurity."
"I think we can safely say that if they'd gone anywhere you'd fall over."
"I woke up this morning and my feathers were huge, much larger than my body so I just haven't got the height to carry it off."
"You look very cute."
"I don't feel 'very cute', it's as though I'm wearing a ball gown. I don't have the freedom of movement I had a few days ago and it's not only the outer layer of feathers, the underneath ones are too long as well."
"Long feathery drawers too hey?"
"I wouldn't know about that as we owlets don't wear such cumbersome things but yes it's all a bit too much in that department."
"Perhaps tomorrow your legs will have grown and all will be back to normal."
"I hope so, I can't move. I'm stuck to the sofa like velcro."
"Shall I pop you on the tiled floor to play? You can glide around with Pixie and her fur covered paws. You could have an Owl & Pussycat version of ' *Strictly Come Dancing* ' which would be nice."
"We're simply a source of entertainment for you aren't we?"
"Of course!"

"You're looking up my knickers!"

"No I'm not, well I am but it was you and the sky I wanted to capture."

"Well couldn't you choose another angle without including my undercarriage?"

"Which angle would you prefer?"

"Above would be a better option, then you could see how glossy my feathers are. I was cleaning them all night while listening to Molly chatting to Darcy about Amex cards."

"So a nice photograph of your back with a gravelled car park as a backdrop? Mmmm that'd work. What's Molly up to then?"

"She was explaining the compound interest on credit cards to Darcy, it seems she's pretty cute when it comes to finance."

"Oh she's cute in every way, he didn't get sucked into her penchant for borrowing did he?"

"No, he spent most of the night intrigued that he had as many wings as he did feet. From what I heard he'd never bothered to count either body part before and was genuinely quite excited."

"Oh bless him, daft as a brush."

"The colour of one too."

"You're not far wrong."

Black Barn Owl or Melanistic Barn Owl is a rarity. Born only in captivity as they'd be killed by their parents in the wild for being the wrong colour these beautiful owls are one in a million.

A little smaller than the normal white Barn owl they also can suffer from poorer eyesight or hearing so they really don't stand a chance of survival in the wild.
Darcy's hearing and eyesight are fine, unfortunately his memory is shocking and each day is a brand new adventure as far as he's concerned.

"Do you come here often?"
"I live here you fool, same as you do. I'm immune to your tomboy charms so cut it out."
"Sorry, I just can't help myself. When I see a beautiful lady I just want to pass the time of day with her."

"Well you can keep your time and your day to yourself, I'm just trying to catch a few rays and ease gently into the morning without any 'how to do' with anyone."

"Bloody hell you're a bit of a handful, I like them feisty!"

"Oh for pity's sake, give it a rest. You're old enough to be my father!"

"Many a fine tune played on an old fiddle my dear."

"Ewww, you dirty old man! Isn't it time you sauntered off into the valley to do whatever you do all day?"

Schminky slowly closed her eyes as if to block out even the merest thought of Nimo's presence, she wasn't known as 'The Princess' for no reason. Her standards had always been so exceptionally high that nothing or nobody was ever going to be good enough.

"Aaah the call of duty does indeed beckon, so many ladies and only one of me. I shouldn't keep them waiting any longer. I must away."

"Before you go, can I ask you something?" Schminky mused for a moment. "You've been done, lost your knackers, had the chop................"

"I know, all the fun with no responsibility. Not like poor old Ted down the road, father to 37 now and he's only two years old! Hasn't a moment to call his own or a cent to his name for that matter. All goes to the various mothers you know, milk and mittens is all they buy. Crying shame. Ted doesn't even have a smoking jacket or cravat to call his own, you know?"

"So is that why all the ladies like you?"

"Partly, but I'd say the real turn on is my singing voice. Since the op' I've been able to hit all the high notes too. I'm like a feline Frankie Valli of the valley., did you see what I did there? Anyway, I must go. Busy day as usual."

"Yeah, you must have them rolling around with mirth."

Nimo jumped down from the bar stool and headed across the garden towards the river, a lolloping saunter at his own speed.

' *Ladies and gentlemen, this is Mambo number five*
A little bit of Monica in my life
A little bit of Erica by my side
A little bit of Rita is all I need
A little bit of Tina is what I see
A little bit of Sandra in the sun
A little bit of Mary all night long
A little bit of Jessica, here I am
A little bit of you makes me your man'

Nimo's relatively melodic voice slowly drifted across the valley, becoming more distant as each minute passed. Schminky had to admit he was a cool character and it was little wonder he had bags under his eyes, maybe he could get surgery for those too.

You came into this world,

On a barmy Autumn day,
As all five of you unfurled,
Laid on my best duvet.
It was a great surprise,
To wake up from fitful sleep,
And stare into her eyes,
Such tiny bundles in a heap.
Tigre and Nimo,
Such typical boys,
Always responsible,
For making the noise.
JD and Fizzy,
And finally Noné,
The first always busy,
The last often lonely.
Four went to homes,
Two did come back.
So the three they would roam,
As a cute little pack.
All loved beyond measure,

The years they have passed,

Memories are treasured,
Ando now Noné's the last.
RIP Nubé (Mum), JD, Nimo, Tigre & Fizzy.

"You look dreadfully uncomfortable Millie."

"Oddly enough I'm not, I feel really quite chilled. I haven't felt so relaxed since I punched Schminky in the face for being downright annoying. That was a good day."

"It's because you're laid on the mica, it's got soporific properties."

"Sopor-what-tic, that sounds dangerous!"

"No, it makes you sleepy."

"I don't need any help in that department, if you haven't noticed I'm a cat. We do sleepy at a professional level. One might say we are the honed athletes of nap taking. Masters of snooze."

"Well there's no doubting that so you'll be extra dozy now."

"Is that dozy as in stupid or dozy as in drowsy?"

"Definitely the drowsy one, your far from stupid."

"So where does this mica stuff hang out when it's not on the kitchen window sill gathering dust?"

"I found it in the garden, the walls of the cave houses in this area are full of it. That's why you always sleep so soundly in a cave bedroom here".

"Cool. I must admit I do zonk out on your bed even if I've been sleeping all day, that must be the reason."

"Or that you've just had your supper."
"A girl's got to keep her strength up, little and often is the key to eating."
"Well you lot certainly do often, we'll leave the 'little' where it is shall we? By rights it should be read as bucket loads at 20 minute intervals if you all had your way."
"What can I say? We're growing cats."
"Mmmm, outwardly expanding cats would be more accurate."

"I wonder what's for breakfast."
"Oh you can bet your bottom dollar it's the same old stuff, she's got no imagination when it comes to menus."
"Oh I don't know, it's not that bad."
"You reckon? Boiled egg, fruit and meat that's all we get and the odd scatter of cat kibble."
"And wiggly worms."
"Yeah I s'pose, wiggly worms. Not enough of those though, she's a bit tight in that department."
"I like breakfast. There's blackberries, raspberries, avocado, kiwi, watercress, and blueberries. I like all of those."
"It's dull though isn't it? Same, old stuff day in, day out."
"Don't forget the mango, papaya and pomegranate. They're lush and I like the bits of chicky as well. What would you have then if you could choose anything at all."

"I want something exotic, an 'amuse bouche' as they say."
"Who says that?"
"Molly the Barn owl says it quite a bit."
"That figures. So what do amuse bouches taste like?
"They're not a food stuff, they're like a little starter to get your taste buds ready for the main course".
"So what would you choose if you could have anything in the whole world?"
"Centipede ankles, I'd like to try those and there'd be plenty of them in a sitting."
"Just the ankles, what about the rest of it?"
"Only the ankles, it's meant to be refined dining not trough chow."
"Like when we eat ants? They don't fill you up but they're fun."
"Yeah, that sort of thing but I don't want ants we can get those anytime. Also the presentation has got to look fantastic, she always falls down on that. No flair at all, she shoves it all in a dish and hopes for the best."
"Oh I've seen fruit and vegetables made to look like flowers on the Internet, tomatoes that look like roses."
"Exactly, a bit of thought should go into it because we eat with our eyes first."
"Our eyes! I've never eaten anything with my eyes, I don't like the sound of that, I don't even like a speck of dust in mine, let alone a banana."
"No you plonker, a meal nicely presented is more appealing than everything chucked together without any thought."
"Ah right, I get you."
"I reckon if she got up earlier rather than languishing in bed until 5am she could knock up a nice breakfast platter. A rocket and watercress base, fresh apricots in 3mm cubes, red pepper strips, avocado mousse, slices of boiled egg and then a multitude of berries scattered on top. A few anchovies well placed would finish it off a treat."
"We don't like anchovies."
"Nobody likes anchovies, they're there for decoration only. Like parsley."
"What about a 'Kitchen Robot'? According to the kookaburras they make anything you want, I'm going to ask her for one because if they've got one we should have one."
"Shhhh I can hear the door, breakfast is about to be served."
"Good morning 'meeeeeries' are you alright, did you sleep well?"
"Yeah, yeah. Less of the chatter, where's the food?"
"Here you go, I managed to find a Savoy cabbage so you've got a bit of that too".
"Oh my God! Savoy cabbage, we've got Savoy cabbage! Life doesn't get any better than this, you can keep your centipede ankles, spider testicles and dung beetle tongues (especially those). Give us the cabbage now!"
Sometimes the most mundane turns into the exotic ;)

"How you doin' mate?".

"Not bad, can't complain. What about you, how's the family?"

"All good fella, little ones are growing. It only seems like last week they were eggs, a lot less hassle when they were mind. Sheila's got her wings full at the moment as they're just fledging, all over the bloody place they are."

"That's kids for you! Never a minute's peace. I said to Daphne only last month,'when this brood has left home, we're down sizing', she wouldn't have it to be though. 'What will I do with all my ornaments?' she said. Take 'em down the bloody charity shop and get shot of them."

"I bet you were popular! Of course you've got that huge Little owl box haven't you? That must take some maintenance and the heating bills must be through the roof."

"It's not just that Bert, the bigger the gaff' the more likely the kids are to come back to live. We had 37 out of the 41 spend Christmas at home, packed to the bloody gunnels we were, could hardly move."

"Where were the others?"

"Gap year from Uni', three of them are over by the window and Tristan was staying with the Hamilton-Smyths in the palm tree."

"What that big one in the corner?"

"Yeah, top notch apparently. I've never been in there, too rich for my blood mate and they only serve cocktails, not my scene at all if you get my drift. I wouldn't swap my perch in 'The Upturned Bucket' for all the mojito's in the world."

"They've always had ideas above their station that lot, all 'lardy-dah' and multiple place settings. We had to go and pick our Shona up from there one day and the missus wanted to have a look inside, glitz and glamour but as Sheila said if you looked closely there was dust everywhere. All 'red hat and no drawers' I reckon."

"You're not wrong! Well I must make a move, I promised to grab some lettuce we're having salads at the moment. Daphne reckons I've piled on the

weight over Winter, I don't think a couple of salads are going to eradicate my beer belly but it keeps her happy."
"Catch you later at the bar then?"
"Wouldn't miss it. It's the only place you can get away from the family."

"Is that for me?"
"No Molly, it's a present for a friend and I'm just going to put it in the car before I forget."
"I can be your friend?" It came across as more of a threat than an invitation.
"That stretches even my imagination Mol' you're not really equipped to be anyone's friend, an associate perhaps but mainly a boss. You're very bossy."
"It's true I do need to take charge occasionally, only because nobody else does and things need doing. If I didn't step up to the mark then goodness knows what chaos would ensue."
"You created a rota for the mews and didn't put yourself on it."
"There wasn't anything for me to do after I'd delegated all the chores and anyway I'm the overseer. That's my position and let me tell you now, it takes up most of my time."

"Barking orders from your perch while you file your talons?".

"Well yes, if I didn't keep some element of control in there it would be bedlam. Anyway, back to the present, what is it?"

"It's a paperweight."

"I need one of those paper weightiness things, urgently."

"You haven't got any paper."

"Well no, but only because you haven't given me any, if you saw fit to dish out some pages then I would need a paperweight to weigh it all down."

"Fortunately I haven't, so you don't. What is it with you lot? Always after something, the meerkats have just asked for a 'Kitchen Robot' . I'm not even sure what that is.
Life isn't about having things, it's about being happy and healthy."

"I'd be happier with a piece of artwork in my bedroom, I asked for that ages ago."

"Molly I'll get around to painting you something as soon as I have a minute, I've been a little busy of late."

"Oh I don't want any of your artwork, that would be like wearing homemade jeans and while Lucy may be content to do so I am most certainly not. No, I want a gallery piece."

"Anything in mind? Van Gogh perhaps, Matisse?"

"I'd like a painting of myself, not an abstract, exact image."

"That's lucky."

"Why do you say that, you haven't got it already?"

"As a matter of fact Mol' I have the very thing.I shall put it up in your bedroom while you're out in the garden, I think you're going to love it."

"I can't wait! Let me out and get on with it."

And that is why Molly has a parrot's mirror in her bedroom, each time she looks in it she sees what she thinks is a perfect painting of herself. Luckily Barn owls are far sighted.

"Morning!"
"Good morning Benny, d'you want a bit of breakfast?"
"Only if you're getting some, I have eaten but you know me, never say no."
"Where's Boris, are you two still flying together?"
"Yes, most of the time, he's taking a break down by the river. He's got it into his head that he's going to go on a fish diet to lose a few grams."
"Still a bit porky then?"
"Well covered he likes to call it."
"Give me a second, I'll go and get you something to eat."

Benny and Boris were the first of that year's Kestrel chicks to be released, they'd fallen out of their nest which had been made in a hole in a stone bridge in the Malaga province and it had been impossible to get them reinstated. They were barely a week old when they arrived.

Both would often pop back for something to eat in the first month which is normal when they're learning to hunt, gradually their visits lessen until all they do is a noisy fly past as they whizz up and down the valley. They still do it now almost three years later.

"Can I ask you something?" Benny said as he cleaned his beak on the branch of the pine tree where he'd taken his lunch.

"Of course you can, whether I can come up with a reasonable answer is another matter, let's give it a go. What's on your mind?"

"This releasing back into the wild thing."

"Yes."

"What are we meant to be doing now we're back in it?" He asked earnestly.

"Well, sort of doing what Kestrels do. Flying around a lot, hunting for things to eat and then sitting in trees to sleep. That more or less covers it as far as I know, not being a Kestrel myself I'm only surmising to be honest."

"Don't we need to find jobs?"

"Well, you've actually got jobs. Because you tend to hunt rodents you're helping the farmers protect their grain crops from being eaten. Also in the valley particularly there are lots of water rats which destroy the earth banks that the irrigation water flows through, by controlling their numbers the land owners aren't having to repair all the holes."

"So should we be getting wages?"

Out of the two of them Benny had always been the brightest and Boris had been aptly named by his rescuer, not that we knew that at the time.

"Your 'wages' are the food you eat I suppose, in an ideal world the farmers and people with allotments would encourage and protect you against any harm. Like a partnership, you help them and they help you."

"Like bees pollinating the trees so that the farmers can harvest the fruit?"

"Yes, very much so. If you didn't do your bit then all the irrigation water would be flooding the fields where it wasn't needed because the water rats would be having a field day making holes all over the place."

"So we don't get hard cash?"

"No, neither do you get soft cash or a bank transfer straight into your account."

"Aah but bees make honey and that gets sold. So in a roundabout way they're earning wages." Benny had almost a valid point.

"Say if you had some money, what would you do with it?"

"I'd create a 'bird wash'. You wouldn't believe how dirty we get flying around, out in Saharan rain. Look what that does to the cars! Filthy stuff."

"Can't you just go to the river and have a quick dunk?"

"I'm talking warm water, a nice smelling soap like lavender and then you could get dried off too so that you don't have to sit around for hours preening. An all in one service".

"It's odd that you've said that. While I was waiting for a delivery lorry to arrive at the local petrol station I saw an Eagle owl fly through the car wash, it wasn't in use but I did think it was strange." This was absolutely true, I had watched a male Eagle owl at dusk fly through the automated car wash.

"Oh typical, somebody's got there first! That's the last time I tell Boris anything, he's got such a big beak."

"How were your customers going to pay for this service? Is it common for birds to have money? I must admit I thought you were a cashless society but I'm starting to wonder now."

"It's unusual but not unheard of. The Choughs and Crows tend to have a bit stashed away but they're tight with it. The Golden eagles obviously have their grants, they have to be seen to have chicks on a regular basis otherwise the government will withdraw the facility but they tend to knock out one a year which helps with cash flow."

"Oh right, well you live and learn. What about having a country style retreat? There's a small hot spring close by that you could utilise. Your customers could bathe in the warm water, slap on a bit of thermally oozed mud and then wash off in the river which is a metre away if that. Dry off in the sunshine and all of it is free to use."

"Already being done by Nora the Moorhen, she's a bit of a battle-axe and guards the spring as if it were her own."

"Well little fella, you're going to have to come up with another idea."

"Yeah, I know. Can I take a little something for Boris to eat, I doubt if he's caught a fish."

"Of course you can, I'll go and get a chick for you. Make sure it's completely defrosted before he starts digging into it, you know what a pig he is but it will be nice and cool for him in this heat."

"How many chicks do you buy each year?"

"About 16,000. Why do you ask?"

"I've had another idea, 'Meals on Wings' or 'Benny's Banquet' which sounds better?"

"Oh hang on a minute!"

Benny flew off towards the river with chick for his brother and a whole new business idea, which I'd apparently be funding.

Over the years there have been several people complain that the birds of prey here eat meat, yes they really have! One lady even suggested that they should feed on nuts and grass.

The birds (including the Kookaburras) eat day-old chicks which come in 8kg cases already frozen. Sadly these chicks are a byproduct of the food industry as they're all males and are of no use, so if they weren't sold to people like ourselves they'd go into landfill.

All birds of prey require meat in various forms, whether it's chicks, rodents, worms or bugs they can't live without it and they also need the roughage of bones, feathers and fur to cast pellets. These are regurgitated and often a bird will cast in the same place everyday so if you find some pellets in the wild and have a trail camera then you should get some great footage.

They're also fascinating to take apart to see what the bird has been eating.

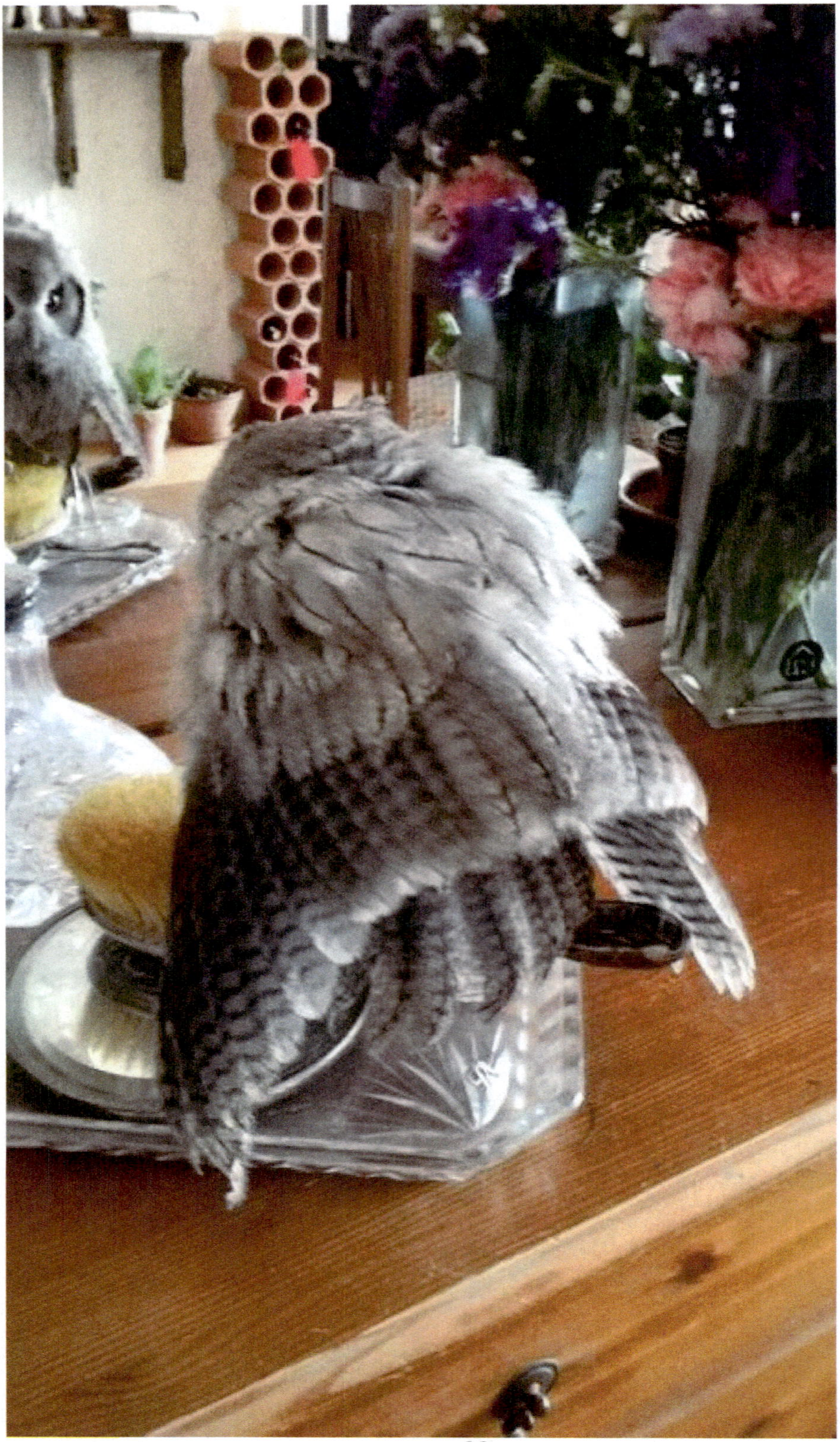

Big owl, small owl. Big owl, small owl.

"What are you doing Mystic?"

"Just testing the theory out."

"Should I ask which theory? As you're perched on my granny's silver hairbrush I'm going to go with Faraday as a wild stab in the dark."

"No, not one of those theories, I could shred most of those in a breath. For example, you do realise there's the (in)famous incompatibility between gravity and quantum mechanics, leading to an essentially infinite number of variants of string theory and other models attempting to reconcile the two don't you?"

"Yes, you've told me before, many times. So, once again, what are you doing?"

"Well they say that my species is known as 'transformer owls' so I was just checking out the levels of transformation I could achieve. I've seen that advert on TV where that yellow car turns into a robot to help a lady with her car which has been in an accident. As yet I haven't altered my appearance substantially to uphold the theory, which is a bit disappointing to say the least."

"Oh bless you. You are a 'transformer owl' but you don't turn into a robot which is a good thing." Having such a highly intelligent being change into a piece of machinery with perhaps super owl strength would have been a worry. Perhaps it would warrant a new chaos theory all of its own.

"Is it? Think of the things I could do."

"Strangely enough that was just what went through my mind, that with a lukewarm feeling of foreboding." I replied. "You and your species are often referred to as transformers due to your amazing ability to go from stick thin when you're frightened to fat little turkey when you're cross, that's where the term has come from."

"I can't go as thin as a stick! As a branch maybe, a stout and sturdy branch but I certainly can't get down to a stick that's impossible."

"I know how you feel Mystic, I can't get down to a size 8 again unless I exist solely on rice paper and leek water. It's 'middle owl spread' sweetie. I strongly believe that my bust and stomach are competing with each other for attention."

"Have you ever considered eating less cake?"

"Thank the lord (Mr. Kipling and his exceedingly small cakes) that it has never even entered my mind as a reason for being generously upholstered."

"You sound like an old sofa."

"I look like an old sofa, faded colours, zippers that have not seen any action in many a long year and my nap's flat. Enough about me though."

We decided that 'stick thin' wasn't for us, we'd concentrate on the more intellectual side of things. Mystic would continue to study anything that took her fancy in the way of Physics and I'd do the same with cook books, cake recipes in particular.

"I am the harbinger of death!"

"Are you Schylar? That's rather a large job for a very small Scops. Who's death?"
"I don't know, we could all go at any moment."
"No, who's death?"
"I've just told you, I don't know."
"Who is death? Not whose death."
"Bloody stupid language it all sounds the same. I don't know who 'Death' is either."
"But as the harbinger you're announcing their arrival surely?"
"What do you want me to say? This is Mr. Death, Mack to his friends?"

"McDeath, is he/she (a bit of controversy for you) Scottish? Only harvests from above   Berwick-upon-Tweed?"

"I wish I hadn't said anything now. I was only joking, I thought it would be funny as I've got a knife behind me. I was trying to be menacing."

"You, menacing? Never, you're far too cute and you also go 'booooop' that's not really a war cry is it? Now Sasa's menacing. Anyway, what are you doing with a knife?"

"It's not mine, I think it belongs to the white budgie. He's been whittling a girlfriend, she doesn't say much."

"Probably can't get a word in edgeways, he talks constantly."

"Would it be OK if I ate a Finch? I thought about it just now but then had the compunction that it really wasn't quite correct so I thought I'd ask first. There's plenty of them in here, Lucy obviously doesn't like them but I reckon I could go one."

"No! It's not a good idea at all, you can move into one of the soft release enclosures now. The aviary is for the Finches and Canaries but it also gives owlets a safe place to practise flying, you were right to ask. It just means that you're growing up and preparing to hunt for yourself which is excellent, when you're released you'll be able to catch food with ease."

"Can I come back and eat them when I'm released?"

"No, you'll be finding allsorts of things to eat in the wild. Scorpions, lizards, beetles and rodents."

"I don't want to leave home, I don't like any of those things you've mentioned and anyway I'm no trouble. Why don't you release Lucy, she's a handful when nobody's looking."

"Lucy's blind so she can't be returned to the wild because she wouldn't be able to hunt, that's why she doesn't try to eat the Finches. You're young, fit and healthy so you must be released to live your life in the wild as nature intended."

"I don't like nature. I like sitting in the house watching the CCTV screen and having my food brought to me at regular intervals, which incidentally could be more regular if you get my drift."

"Well, you can always come back and visit or pop in for something to eat. Pippin comes back each year for the Summer."

"Can I still come in the house?"

"If you want to, that's not a problem but I think you'll love flying around the valley and that will be far more interesting for you."

"I could fly in front of the cameras and you could watch me on the CCTV!"

"Now there's a good idea. In the meantime let's get you out of the aviary before Mr.Mack Death does actually put in an appearance."

I was a dancer you know, back in the day. Not of a frivolous nature you understand, although my parents did frown upon my choice of career when I told them. They saw me more as settling down with some nice fellow and having a family but the bright lights called my name, I lived to dance.

From the moment I could walk I would strutt or shimmy, my siblings thought me most odd but I cared not for their contentious discourse, I was different. I had plans, dreams and within weeks I'd left home to seek a stage bright enough for me to perform on.

I do believe we attract what we desire, if indeed that desire is strong enough. A lovely couple adopted me, they wanted my company on their adventures and although I was born in Great Britain, I travelled Europe with them and finally came to rest in Spain. The land of Flamenco, one of the most passionate and theatrical dances of them all. They however, were not that enamoured with the area and one night they left without saying a word, I was out taking in the evening air, listening to the frogs and crickets murmuring in the final hour of dusk.

Of course I was bereft, lonely and somewhat frightened but some neighbours offered me a safe haven by leaving a bedroom window open each night and preparing wonderful feasts. Such kindly souls, they had a dog which they favoured but I didn't concern myself with popularity. I could concentrate on my forte without distraction.

My niche was found, a small but exclusive venue close by. Of course I had to start as all dancers do, in the chorus line but I shone! Within weeks I was given my own spotlight and quickly a loose assemblage of diverse groups would attend my performances. Silk ribbons would be cast before me which I'd wear with a hint of derring-do for my gentlemen admirers. Please don't think I walked the road of being a harlot, not at all. I was chaste, pure and of course as white as the driven snow.

I was idolised, in fact that's where my name came from "I adore her" they'd say so of course 'Adorable Dora' I became. Invites would pour into my dressing room, one party after another and I would try to attend them all to dance the night away. Gentlemen would ask me to dine with them but I was too absorbed in my career, there was no more space for anything other than dance, my one and only love.

Sadly as the years passed the punishing nature of the art took its toll on my body, my knees and feet ached, I could no longer throw myself into a routine with the intensity that it deserved. It was time to hang up my ribbons and shoes, to retire with dignity.

Sitting in the bedroom that I had lived in for several years I wished for some company, although the neighbours who had saved me were so very charming they still had their dog. I needed stimulation, I'd always been so active and had a great many acquaintances that now life seemed a little drab.

And so it was that a lady came to collect me. It transpired that she had recently lost a cat of many years so wanted a mature companion, I was delighted. Such a silly-billy was I not to imagine that there'd be other cats, it came as quite a shock to meet owls and meerkats too but I took it in my stride. They were friendly enough although lacking in fine education and often basic manners, a little on the common side if I were to speak plainly.

I have made a very comfortable life here, I don't of course eat with the others, much preferring my food to be served on my own bone china dish in the kitchen window sill. I simply will not yield on that. I have my own chair. It's Victorian with a beautiful hand embroidered cushion, a little touch of luxury I always appreciate. In the mornings I sit in the sun after breakfast, often reminiscing of days gone by. I can't complain, my life has been full to the brim with adventure and now in my twilight years (a true lady never discusses such things) I have everything I could wish for.

    I even have 'Alexa' by my chair, when all is quiet I ask her to play music of my era while I doze and dream of times gone by.

"Can I touch your feet?"
"Why?"
"I want to see if they're real."
"Of course they're real, they're not pretend feet.'Oh I'll put on my imaginary feet this morning' says nobody ever!"
"It was more your legs than your feet to be accurate, you've got leggings on."
"Leggings? I haven't got leggings on, they're just my feathers."
"Why have you got feathers on your legs, I thought you'd just have skin like chickens and ducks do."

    "I don't know, it's just the way we're made. You've got hairy legs. Why is that, you can't say, can you?"

    "I'd look ridiculous with bare legs plus I'd get cold when I went out into the snow."

    "You've never even seen snow, let alone been out in it."

    "Well no, but as a Maine Coon I'm hardwired for snow. I was born to run around in snow, that's why I've even got hairy feet unlike the rest of the cats. Give me a snow drift and I could walk on top of it easily, the rest would sink in."

"I think we've covered the white stuff copiously don't you? Maybe I've got leg feathers to keep me warm too. Have you ever thought of that?"

"You do nothing but sit by the fire or on top of a candle lamp, you've never known a millisecond of chilliness. The whole house comes to a standstill if your candle's gone out in the aviary, a mad dash ensues to relight the T-light before you can experience less than 15 degrees."

"Perhaps my species will evolve then and we'll all have bare legs."

"I don't think one owl will effectively change the appearance of a whole species to be brutally frank, but if for some reason you lot do start appearing un-feathered in the knee department one would ask oneself, would anybody really notice?"

"One would, would one? I'll have you know I actually have very long legs, not just knees."

"You must have a low undercarriage then, all I can clearly see are your ankles and talons. I remembered you had knees that's why I mentioned them, I can't actually see them."

"I do not want to discuss my undercarriage, low or otherwise with you. I may be carrying an extra gram or two but it's Winter and everyone knows you need to feed up against the cold weather. Please don't start with the snow talk again."

"I wouldn't dream of it. So can I touch your feet now."

"Oh go on then, if it'll make you happy."

Maine Coon cats don't meow at all; they chirp. Why did this breed evolve to make such an odd sound? No one knows for sure, but it's yet another way that the Maine Coon is different from all other cats. The sound itself might take a little getting used to. It has a trilling quality that some people might find maddening. On the other hand, Maine Coon owners promise that their cats' sounds are what make them so endearing.

Cats generally love to be high. The cliché of the firefighter rescuing cats from trees originates from this very fact: cats love heights. They will climb up the tallest trees and scale up the highest steps just so they can be above everything. It could very well be that the reason why cats love heights is because they love to jump. Maine Coon cats are the exact opposite of the typical, again. They absolutely hate heights. While there's no governing evidence or scientific study that has proven this, Maine Coon owners will tell you just out of observation. These cats like to stay low on the ground for some reason. Again, it could very well be an evolved characteristic that we're not sure what the reason is for.

These animals are loving and extremely affectionate. They don't like confrontation, so they'll do very well with other animals in the home. You'll be short on the typical feistiness that comes with pet cats. With the Maine Coon cat, you'll only have lots of loving and attention. Don't worry if you can't give it constantly either. Maine Coon cats are just as laid back as they are loving. They know how to entertain themselves until you come back to snuggle them again.

"Dad, what you doin'?"

"Just having a wee son, you carry on playing. I won't be long."

"Dad, you still weeing?"

"Yes little mate, go and get your toys out and we can play in the sunshine." Florian does as his dad suggests and scampers into the bunker to gather his favourite toys. Re appearing he finds his dad just as he left him.

"Dad! Are you ever going to stop?"

"I hope so Floz' otherwise I'll turn into a crisp and blow away," Alessi chuckled at the joke he'd made.

"Don't do that dad, I don't want you to go."

"When you're my age son, perhaps you'll remember this conversation. Dad's pee for a ridiculously long time, it gives us an opportunity of peace (normally) from the family first thing in the morning. A chance to think about the day ahead, what needs to be done and also empties the ole' tanks in readiness for filling back up again. As a father we often get bogged down with work and problems, it's always good to put things into perspective and see the bigger picture. Some things don't seem half so bad once you've had a few minutes to fathom out what to do, I do some of my best thinking when I'm weeing you know. Solve issues, come up with ideas, count ants, all sorts of things go through my mind. Like why your mother insists on eating all the avocado and then moans about not losing the baby weight she put on. Why do the Kookaburras have those huge snappy beaks and why do they have to poke them into everyone else's business."

"We heard that!" Came a resounding reply from the Kookaburras in unison.

"They've obviously got bloody big ears to match their beaks, you'd think they'd hardly have ears at all considering how loud they talk to each other."

"Dad".

"In a minute fella, hold your horses."

"But dad!"

"Right I'm all ears, what's up?"

"You've been peeing in the entrance to the bunker, it's all run down into the kitchen. Mum's going to go absolutely spare when she finds out."

"Why didn't you tell me before?"

"I didn't like to interrupt, you always say that we should touch your hand when we want to speak while you're doing something and once you've finished, we can then say whatever it was that we needed to tell you. I wasn't keen on touching your hand so I thought I'd just wait patiently."

"You're a good boy Florian, your manners are coming along beautifully. Don't worry about your mother, I'll tell her you had a little accident. Well you and your sister."

"I will save you!"

"Cheers Fuji, but I'm just using the food processor. I don't think I'm in any immediate danger."

"It's too loud and dangerous, turn it off."

"What?"

"TURN IT OFF!"

"I didn't realise you could shout in capital letters, what a fine pair of lungs you have."

"That's better. Are you in one piece, no fingers missing?"

"All present and correct, thank you."

"So I can fold up and stand down now?"

"Yep, you've done a sterling job keeping me from the marauding tendencies of the machine. Where were you before you swooped in here?"

"I was on top of the curtain rail making faces at Pixie, she's never worked out that if she jumped onto the dresser she could catch me."

"She's too well behaved to do anything like that."

"Or too lazy."

"Good point well made. Do you want to go outside? The sun's come out a bit so it should be warm enough."

"What and leave you alone in the kitchen, doing goodness knows what with all these gadgets. I wouldn't be doing my job properly if I were to do that, what would they all say?"

"What's your job then? Apart from being a bitey nuisance."

"I didn't mean to bite your lip that time, Jees will you stop bringing that up it was ages ago!" Fuji at this point, stomped across my shoulders in disgust at my constant reminder of when she had clamped her beak onto my bottom lip with such vigour, I subsequently spent a couple of days with a semi 'trout pout'. One friend even asked which salon I'd gone to for Botox, clearly to make a mental note, to not go there herself.

"I've popped my name down for security, I thought it would be an ideal career for me. I'm sharper than a badger, smart as a walnut and my vision is second only to a tea cup."

"You're as mad as a hatter though."

"Oh yes, as mad as a hatter. I missed that one out."

"So your speciality is going to be close personal protection going by your activities this morning. Like a bodyguard?"

"I thought that would make the most sense, there's the dogs with their barks to do the rough stuff. I'm more of the thinking woman's security, I can accessorise any outfit. Let's face it I'm not exactly colourful, more camouflage if the truth be told."

"Do you think there's a need for you to be a bodyguard though? It's not as if anyone comes to the house uninvited is it?"

"Do you know, I put this to myself when I first came up with the idea. Call it risk assessment if you like."

"OK I will."

"It's not the weirdos and freaks out there wanting to break in to do harm. They're not the problem, it's those already here that pose the threat."

"Oh we can all sleep soundly now can't we?! Who's the nutter then? Who's wandering around with a machete in the dead of night? Slipping poison into the coffee? Broken glass into the food?"

"It's you."

"Hang on a minute, I would never do anything of the sort!"

"No, you're not a danger to anyone else but yourself. Who would imagine that the best way to retrieve something from the Meerkats enclosure was to lean so far into it that she broke a rib?"

"Mmmmm."

"On that same note, jumping off the ruin garden fracturing a heel. Ring any bells? And so it goes on, but not now I'm in charge. If I see you doing anything utterly stupid I shall tell you, thus preventing anymore accidents."

"You're going to be run off your talons Fuji, I wish you the very best of luck".

Little owls have an awful lot to say and they're fantastic mimics, with over forty different calls or sounds they possess the widest vocabulary of the owl world. It appears the larger the owl the lesser the range of chit chat.

Fuji can mimic the Barn owls swearing, miniature chickens and heart monitors quite happily for hours at a time. She's struggling to master Kookaburra though.

"So if quantum mechanics is as you said, the study of very small things, are you one of the small things that scientists have been studying?"
"No, of course not. They study electrons, protons, neutrons, and other more esoteric particles such as quarks and gluons. Not Little owls."
"Gluons sound like fun, are they like eyes and noses you can stick on things? Like a Mr.Potato head?"
"You really don't get any of this do you? Gluons are an elementary particle…………Hang on a minute, do I sense she's seen us?"
"Yep, she's got her mobile poised for a photo opportunity. Say fleas!"
"Fleeeeaassss!"
      "Has she gone?"
      "No, she's loitering in case we do anything cute."
      "Better dumb down the conversation a bit, I don't think she'd be able to grasp the content without running to the hills screaming in disbelief that we, or more accurately I have a good basic knowledge of physics."

"Does she do that then, run to the hills screaming? I've seen her fall down the hill carrying one of the meerkats, right old tumble and then a loud thump as she fell off the edge."

"Yeah, I heard about that. The Kookaburras said that she held Peachey aloft as if she were a fine glass of wine, wouldn't have spilt a drop. I believe humans put quite a value on the alcoholic contents of a vessel, you can get bottles of the stuff that cost as much as a zillion, billion Euro you know."

"No! Is that expensive?"

"Oh yes, it's as much as a tea towel with a picture of Looe harbour printed on it."

"I'm glad you've mentioned that. Is that where tea comes from? I know the coffee comes out of a jar on the shelf because she makes two of those a day. It's always a good bet that she may want some milk from the pantry in which case we can storm the area for snacks while she's trying to make her drink, so I've seen her creating coffee lots of times but never the tea."

"You're absolutely correct Pixie. I think the type of tea towel plays quite an important part, she only uses one's with scenes of Yorkshire on them for ordinary tea. Then there's the Taj Mahal for chai, various fruit printed towels which are self explanatory and a tea towel which must have Spynx on it for ginger tea, I can't think of anything else that's ginger so it must be of him. Either that or she puts his tail in the cup, he's always in the kitchen."

"Does the whole thing go in the cup?"

"No, she just uses a corner I think. Rotates it each time somebody wants some tea and then hangs it up to dry off, ready for next time."

"You can understand why visitors only have the one cup really, can't you?"

"How are you today then Nelly?"
"Alright."
"Any plans, thoughts or movement on your agenda?"
"Nope."

"So you're more than happy to sit on the dining table all day waiting for your twenty minute feeds?"

"Yep."

"How about, getting up and having a walk around. You really should get some form of exercise otherwise your species will evolve to have no feet at all which would be a pity, you've got lovely feet."

"We Nightjars mainly sit or fly. As I haven't learnt to fly I'm concentrating on sitting at the moment."

"You've fledged Nelly so you can fly, all your feathers are in place, it's just a case of lifting off."

"Prefer sitting."

"And eating?"

"Yeah, eating's good."

"You're not that keen on talking though or of course moving in anyway."

"Why waste energy?"

"Well there is that. You know you're going to be released next week don't you?"

"Yep."

"Are you worried about it?"

"Nope."

"Have you got anything on your mind at all?"

"What do I look like?"

"You look like a Nightjar, a fully fledged, able to fly off and start your adult life sort of Nightjar."

"I don't know what one of them is. Do I look like a bit of scrubby earth?"

"Well yes, your camouflage is amazing. You'll be invisible on the ground."

"That's alright then, when you let me go I can sit around out there too."

"You'll be flying around hunting for insects, there won't be time to sit and stare into the middle distance. Then you'll meet a mate, lay some eggs which will hatch into chicks and you'll have to look after them so they grow up to be strong, healthy Nightjars."

"That's all a bit hectic."

"Well, it's sort of in your job description. You're hardwired to do all these things to keep your species alive."

"I'm not fussed you know, there's plenty of us around, it's not as if I'm one of only a handful left. I reckon I'll stay here. I haven't any great ambition like becoming Prime Minister or anything."

"Maybe you should consider that position, Nelly, you could show them what hard work really looks like."

"I'll think about that. Any food going?"

Nelly was successfully released the following week.

Nightjars are nocturnal birds and can be seen hawking for food at dusk and dawn. With pointed wings and a long tail their shape is similar to a kestrel or cuckoo. Their cryptic, grey-brown, mottled, streaked and barred plumage provides ideal camouflage in the daytime.

Due to their elusive nocturnal habits, nightjars have been the basis for many myths and legends. In many European countries, the nightjar is known as a 'goatsucker' after its Latin name, as they were believed to feed from goats due to the fact that they were often found in close proximity to livestock; we now know that the attraction is the invertebrates associated with livestock.

"Good gracious, what on earth have you done to your hair?!"
"It's drizzling outside, you know it always becomes a little odd in damp weather. I just popped Lucy into the aviary and it's horrible out there."

"You look as though you've spent the night in a typhoon rather than a few seconds in a modicum of slightly moist air."

"Cheers Fuji, tell it how it is hey?"

"I couldn't let it pass, you look like Medusa with the heaving pile of snakes on her head, apart from yours are multi coloured with grey go faster stripes."

"You really are full of compliments today aren't you? I'll have you know I inherited Great Granny's red afro hair gene, well a smidge of it. So no matter what I do, if it gets wet it reverts back to………..."

"Chaos by the looks of things! Has it ever, even seen a comb?"

"Yes, thank you very much. I waved it around vaguely, it became tangled so I put it back in the drawer. It's OK for you, you've got feathers, if you get wet they don't change into anything other than wet feathers. Whereas hair does odd things, it goes curly, straight or frizzy. We humans spend millions on hair products to try and control or create the desired style and then there's dryers, tongs, plates, curlers etc."

"So when are you going to buy some to tame that nest of Vipers? You've got something sticking out as well, a blue stick or ……………..Oh goodness you've got a pen in there! Did you know or has it crept in at some point to find a safe haven?"

"I put it in my hair earlier, I don't have the right sort of ears to put pens or pencils behind but up there works like a dream."

"What else can you accommodate in the mass?"

"Artists brushes, pens and pencils really. I haven't ventured towards testing anything else out."

"What about mice, have you got any of those lurking in there?"

"No, that would be wholly unpleasant."

"Pity that, you could defrost them and carry so much more at feeding time. Might be worth considering you know, multi tasking and all that plus you'd have a purpose for that big mop."

"Cheers for that Fuji, I'll give it my full consideration at some point. Now if you don't mind I need to find out where the chickens have been laying their eggs, we're running a bit short and the Meerkats are complaining."

"I know where I'd look first!"

People often ask where the names come from for the birds and animals, most have meanings of some description and with Pippin and Fuji they were both named after apples.

Little owl chicks remind me of Crab apples in their shape and quite often they're 'crabby' in nature when they first come in, Pippin never really lost that element of her character.

"I'm Mata Hari of the cat world."

"Gosh, are you? Where do you get these ideas from? Mata Hari indeed, do you know why she became famous?"

"Yes, she was a spy. Just like me."

"Well there's a little more to the story than that, she was a Dutch exotic dancer, the perfect cover to be a spy and considered to be quite a looker. So with her minimalist costumes and pleasant demeanour she was of course quite a hit with the gentlemen. They'd tell her their wartime secrets and she'd pass those on to her contacts."

"So a snitch and a spy?"

"Well it sort of goes with the territory really, there's no point being a spy unless you use the information you've gathered I suppose. Otherwise you'd just be an observer of things that happen, not quite so glamorous."

"I'm the 'observer' of not very much with you standing in front of me."

"Can you not go somewhere else for your mission? I'm trying to get the sofa cushions back into the covers and in an ideal world there wouldn't be the added hassle of having you in amongst it all."

"Why don't you zip me up in here? That way I could frighten the life out of everyone by suddenly coming alive like a big blue, crushed velvet zombie."

"Although a very tempting idea I'd rather just get the sofa back together, why don't you go into the olive grove and spy on GaGa? She's always up to mischief and then you can come back and report her antics like a proper spy would."

"Nah, I've gone off the idea now and anyway I watch Ga' everyday. What happens in the valley, stays in the valley, she says."

Millie eventually decided to come out of the fitted covers and thought the best plan of campaign was to have a third breakfast and then a snooze, she would need her strength to take up skateboarding that evening.

Having a Maine Coon is not like having your standard, everyday variety of cat. It's more akin to having a highly intelligent, slightly gangly, obsessive compulsive fairy with great big hairy feet.

Cat behaviour only makes up about 30% of a Maine Coon, they have the same fundamental likenesses, ears, tail, fur and claws but that's where it stops. Only the basics a

"What's up Pixie?"

"I can't fold up, I've been trying all morning but I haven't got enough hinges. My legs just don't do what I want them to do, I'm like a child's drawing. I have no knees."

"You do have knees, you banana! And elbows and ankles for that matter, you're not missing any integral parts of your skeleton."

"Why can't I do the arm folding thing like the others do? Their tiny little paws tuck underneath them so tidily, look at my legs! They're always out in front, always in my eye line they won't collapse down. I can't put them away".

"You're not made quite the same way Pix' you're a bit more industrial. You're made for snow, not that we get any of that usually but that's your forte. If we had snow drifts the rest of the cats would sink to the bottom of them and have to be dug out whereas you would walk across the drift easily because of your……."

"Big feet, you were going to say I've got big feet weren't you?"

"I was actually going to say furry feet, big hadn't entered my mind". It had though because they are of a generous size.

"My tail is too big as well. The others wander around with their tails in the air, a flick here and there or a question mark shape when they're being nosey. I can't lift mine above my bum, if I do my back aches."

"Instead of dwelling on what you can't do, why not think about what you can do that the others can't. Who can jump from the floor to on top of the dresser? Or jump over the sofa onto the coffee table?"

"I can, I suppose."

"Also who has a ready made pillow to lay their head on? Wherever you want to sleep you've always got your tail with you to keep you warm and provide a comfy cushion. The rest of the cats with their little stringy tails don't have that luxury at all."

"I'm really special because I have to go to the vets quite often too, they don't".

"That's mainly due to what you tend to eat Pix', the mistletoe berry from a Christmas bouquet wasn't your finest hour and I think I paid for a national debt that day at the veterinary hospital".

"It was a day out though, I was surprised that there wasn't more traffic in a big city like Granada".

"Yeah, odd that given it was Christmas day!"

"So getting back to my legs, do they look silly like this?"

"No they look perfectly fine, you're a very beautiful little girl with a bit more growing left to do so it will all fall into place soon. Don't worry about it and don't listen to what others say, they're only jealous".

"OK, I think I need to have forty winks now. It's very tiring being me all the time."

Printed in Great Britain
by Amazon